An Unexpected Spark

Delaney Diamond

Garden Avenue Press

An Unexpected Spark by Delaney Diamond

Garden Avenue Press

Atlanta, Georgia

978-1-946302-32-8 (Ebook edition)

978-1-946302-33-5 (Paperback edition)

www.delaneydiamond.com

Chapter 1

Tallulah

"Mom?"

My daughter called to me from the front of the house where I'd just heard the door open and close.

"I'm in the kitchen," I called back.

Slowly, I poured my homemade kombucha into a swing-top glass bottle using a funnel. I kept the drinks in a small refrigerator at Simply Well, my herbal store and wellness center. I usually sold out every week, and regular customers often asked me to make more. Maybe one day I would, but for now, small batches were enough to keep me busy, adding a few extra dollars to my bottom line.

Blossom walked in as I poured the last drop of golden liquid and closed the swing top.

"How was your date?" I asked.

She appeared in front of me, a curious smile on her face. Her skin was a couple of shades lighter than mine, and her natural curls were cut low on her oval face, giving her a modern, self-assured look. She seemed happy, but also like someone holding onto a juicy secret.

"Must have been good," I remarked, tugging off my gloves.

"I'm getting married!" she blurted.

Huh?

Stunned, I stared at her. "M-married? To who?"

"Manuel, Mom! Who do you think? The guy I've been dating."

Blossom and I had a good relationship and told each other everything. After her father and I divorced when she was in middle school, we became closer. I knew all about her struggles with puberty, her crushes—including the one on her science teacher in tenth grade that thankfully only lasted a few months before she moved on to a boy her own age.

I distinctly remember our candid conversations about sex and being safe, and when she was ready, I took her to the doctor for birth control. She never hid bad grades from me, and I knew about her serious boyfriends. All two of them.

I knew they were serious because she brought them home to meet me. Since I hadn't met Manuel, I had assumed they were in a casual relationship.

"Yes, you did tell me about him, but I had no idea the relationship was this far along. You met right before graduation, didn't you?" I successfully kept the alarm out of my voice.

She nodded vigorously. "In February. One minute we were sharing a meal in the park beside our favorite food trucks, and the next we were inseparable. It's been a whirlwind."

I was normally a chill, go-with-the-flow kind of person, but my laid-back personality flew out the window when the topic of marriage came up. If nothing else, I had instilled in my daughter the importance of picking the right life partner. Yet she had met this young man her last semester in college—only

four months ago—found out they were both from Ellington, Michigan, and now they were engaged.

Whirlwind was an understatement.

It's possible I hadn't been paying as much attention to her relationship as I usually did since I was dealing with uncertainty about the future of my wellness center. A company out of Texas had recently bought the building where I leased space, and I and the other shop owners were concerned about what that meant for the future of our businesses.

"Well, congratulations. Let me see the ring."

She grimaced. "Don't be weird, okay? I don't have a ring yet. Tonight we had takeout at his apartment—our favorite meal from the Korean place up the street. He cut a strip from the takeout bag and taped it around my finger. It has our initials on it—M & B."

She proudly extended her hand and stroked the white paper with black writing, her face fixed in an adoring expression, as if it were a piece of fine jewelry. My God, she was a goner. Manuel hadn't planned, and my daughter said yes anyway. This was so unserious.

"Oh." My mind raced for something positive to say.

"It's the thought that counts," Blossom hastily explained. "We're going to pick out rings together. Later."

Uh-huh.

I cleared my throat, opting for tact instead of chastisement. "Blossom, my love, marriage is a big deal, and you've only known this boy a short time. He didn't buy—"

"He's not a *boy*. He's an adult, like me," she corrected.

"Yes, you're both adults, but you're young. I assume he's also twenty-two?"

She nodded, crossing her arms over her chest, a move her father used to make that drove me up the wall. It meant she was shutting down and wouldn't absorb the words of wisdom I was about to drop into the conversation.

"You're both young. You have your whole lives ahead of you. You haven't found a job yet, and marriage is a big step with lifelong implications."

"I was hesitant to tell you about my engagement because I knew you'd do this. I knew you'd advise me against marriage."

"I'm not advising you against getting married. I'm telling you why you shouldn't be thinking about getting married *right now*, especially to someone you barely know."

"I *know* him. Let's be real—it's not about how well we know each other. You hate the institution of marriage!" my daughter exclaimed.

"I do *not*," I denied.

Since she had always been open and honest with me growing up, I had extended the same courtesy to her. She knew when I started dating after her father and I split, but I never introduced her to any of my lovers. I never considered them permanent.

I wanted to get married again. Truly I did. I had loved being married when my marriage was good. Her father, Karl, God rest his soul (he's not dead, but I like saying that), had been the epitome of a "good husband" when we first married. Those first few years were what I wanted to experience again.

Having someone to talk to and laugh with. Having a partner to tell my secrets, my fears, my aspirations. Someone I was allowed to make mistakes in front of without judgment. Having a date to functions, if only to watch a movie by my favorite actor or attend a comedy show on the weekend. Having someone to cuddle with and make love to. I have to give Karl his props—the man could *put it down* in the bedroom.

To this day, I still missed his tongue. And his penis. *Damn.*

"Mom, I want you to be happy for me, even though you hate the institution of marriage."

"I do not hate the institution of marriage, Blossom," I said between gritted teeth. "Uncross your arms, because you're not listening to me."

She did as I asked. She might be an adult, but she was still my daughter, and she listened to me. Most of the time.

"I do not hate marriage."

"Then why haven't you remarried in all this time?"

"Usually you have to be asked."

"You've had plenty of relationships."

"Plenty is an exaggeration, but none of those men asked me, and to be honest, I never wanted to marry any of them."

"Do you miss Dad?" she asked tentatively.

"No!" I only missed his tongue. And his penis. "I would love to get married again if the right man comes along, but I'm forty-seven. The chances of that happening are getting slimmer as I age."

How did we get off on this tangent? We were supposed to be steering her away from poor decision-making.

I gently gripped her arms. "My love, I want the best for you, and you shocked me with your announcement."

"I know, but I'm excited, and like I said, everything happened so fast. We connected right away, and it's been that way ever since."

"Does he have a job?" I asked.

"Yes. He has a job at Phase One Bank, where his father works."

"Good," I said, resting my hands on my hips.

"*I* need to find a job."

"Ellington is booming. I'm sure you'll find work soon. Until then, you're welcome to work with me."

"Um... I'm gonna keep pounding the pavement. I want a job in my field."

I didn't take offense. She had worked with me in high school and summers home from college when she didn't travel with her friends. It was understandable that she wanted to do something else, particularly since she'd gotten a degree in cybersecurity. I assumed finding a job would be easy for her, but she was having a hard time. I suspected her lack of prospects was because she was a woman.

"If you change your mind, let me know," I told her. "When do I get to meet Manuel? I don't know anything about him, and I'm sure he'd like to meet me too."

"I'm glad you brought that up because he does want to meet you, and I want to meet his father. He said his father is kind of square and rigid, which reminded me of Dad," Blossom said with a laugh. "We thought it would be a good idea for the four of us to have dinner together."

I picked up two bottles of kombucha and placed them in the pantry, where I'd leave them for a few days before refrigerating them. "When were you thinking?"

"Friday night."

"This Friday? That's only a few days away." I picked up two more bottles.

"We felt the sooner the better."

We.

She was already speaking in the plural. I had to meet this young man before he took complete control of her brain cells. Meeting his father at the same time would be good too, so I'd have a sense of the type of family she was marrying into.

"Tentatively scheduled for seven o'clock at Knife & Fork," Blossom said.

Knife & Fork was a popular steak restaurant that I had never been to. I no longer ate red meat—or pork—so it was the kind of place I hadn't been anxious to visit. I'd have to check the menu beforehand to see what dishes I could eat.

"Got it."

She smiled. "And Mom, be nice, okay?"

"I'm always nice." This time I was offended.

She looked at her fake-ring-piece-of-paper thingy and then lifted her gaze. "Are you happy for me?"

For a moment, she was my little girl, seeking my approval. Not the adult she insisted was ready for marriage. I had reservations, and I wanted the best for her.

I placed my hands on her arms again. "If this is what you want, and he's a good man, I'm very happy for you. Love is a beautiful thing if you can find it."

"It is what I want, and he is a good man."

I'll be the judge of that.

I pulled her into my arms. "Then I can't wait to meet him."

I kissed her cheek, and a smile spread across her face. "I'll call him now and let him know we're confirmed for Friday night."

She rushed out of the kitchen, and I started cleaning up. It was almost my bedtime, but I had a feeling my mind would be preoccupied with the engagement. I wouldn't be able to rest until I had met Blossom's fiancé and determined if he was good enough for my daughter.

Chapter 2

Jamison

"W*hat do you mean you're getting married?"* I panted, staring at my son in disbelief. Sweat dripped down the sides of my face from the incline and speed of the treadmill I was running on before work.

For years, I had regularly gone to the gym and still did, but lately, I had been struggling with insomnia and often woke up early. Instead of lying in bed doing nothing, I had placed a treadmill in my bedroom and added an extra forty-five minutes of exercise to my day.

Manuel gave me one of his exasperated looks. "You know what getting married means. You were married once, remember?"

Not only did my son look a lot like his Mexican mother—inheriting her swarthy skin, curly black hair, and dark eyes—he also tended to have her snark.

Yes, I knew exactly what marriage was, which was why I was alarmed. His mother and I didn't last because, quite frankly, we were incompatible and ignored our differences because we thought we were in love. Although I looked forward to the day Manuel got married and I became a grandfather, I had not expected marriage to happen so soon. He was practically still a kid, and worse, he was engaged to a young woman I had never met.

"When did this happen?"

He beamed at me as he recalled the moment. "Last night, which is why I couldn't wait to come by and tell you."

Manuel no longer lived with me. As soon as he received his first paycheck, he moved out and leased his own apartment. I wasn't one of those parents who believed in kicking a kid out as soon as they became an adult. I was very familiar with financial struggle and had suggested he live with me a while longer to save money, but he claimed he needed privacy. At least he had been sensible about his choice, finding a moderately priced apartment in a good neighborhood.

"Asking Blossom to marry me was completely spontaneous. I wanted an elaborate proposal, but I ended up popping the question after we ate dinner at my place."

I wiped sweat from my face with my towel. "Who is this young lady?" I panted.

"I've told you about her. *Blossom.* We met at school."

I did remember him talking about a young woman named Blossom. I had no idea they were so serious. "Have you met her parents?"

"Not yet."

Agitated, I stopped the treadmill and slowed to a walk as the speed decreased and the incline lowered. Stepping off the machine, I puffed out a tired breath. "You never went to her father and asked his permission to marry his daughter?"

"Dad, come on, that's an old-fashioned idea. People my age rarely do that. Besides, her father lives in Georgia, but her mother lives here."

Maybe I hadn't raised him so well after all. I wasn't happy. This young woman agreed to marry my son without meeting anyone from his family and vice versa.

Red flag.

What was wrong with young people these days? You raise them one way and they go completely against your teachings. It's as if my son wanted to give me a heart attack.

"Of course, you know, I have to meet Blossom."

"I want you to meet her, and she wants to meet you. We figured it would be a good idea for the four of us—me and you, she and her mother—to have dinner together. I suggested Friday night."

"This Friday night?"

"Yes. After work."

I mentally ran through my calendar. "That's doable. I need to check with Mindy first before I confirm," I said, referring to my executive assistant.

"I left her a message, so you should have an answer when you go in this morning."

My son and I worked together. He was a junior credit analyst, and I was a commercial banker at Phase One Bank, a large outfit in the Midwest. I specialized in negotiating and closing commercial loans and spent a lot of time marketing our services to potential clients. My job wasn't glamorous, but it was exciting work, at least for me. Second only to sex, which I hadn't been getting much of these days.

"Where did you want to have dinner?" I asked.

"How about Knife & Fork?"

"Why there? It's expensive."

Manuel rubbed his hands together. "I want to make a good impression on Blossom's mom, so I don't want to go to any old place."

"Knife & Fork is one of the most expensive restaurants in

town, and on a Friday night, they'll probably be booked. There are other options."

"Can we at least try?" Manuel asked.

I sighed. "All right, Knife & Fork it is. Are you sure they can afford it?"

I glanced absentmindedly at the activity tracker on my wrist. Heart rate looked good. Calories burned, good. Had my son not interrupted me, I would have burned more calories.

I suddenly realized the room was oddly quiet and looked at Manuel. He looked at me.

"No," I said.

"Come on, Dad. Don't be cheap for once in your life."

"Cheap? Is that what you call being sensible about your finances?" I demanded. "*Cheap* covered the expenses your scholarship didn't and allowed you to graduate from college loan-free."

He sighed dramatically. "You go to Knife & Fork all the time with clients."

"Yes, with *clients*. To impress them. I don't pay out of my own pocket for those meals. They're a business expense."

"Well, we're trying to impress Blossom and her mother."

His logic was terribly flawed.

"You mean *you're* trying to impress them, with my money. What does Blossom's mother do?"

"She owns a store where she sells herbal supplements and stuff like that. There's also a yoga studio in the back of the store."

Great. She probably wouldn't appreciate a place like Knife & Fork. Probably didn't eat meat. "And Blossom?"

He hesitated, which meant I wouldn't like the answer.

"She's looking for a job in cybersecurity, and she's had some interviews."

Another red flag.

Once again, I was disappointed. Granted, my son got his foot in the door of the bank because of me, but that was beside the point. I had warned him years ago that any woman he married should have a job of some kind. I didn't care if she walked dogs part-time—which in some parts of the country could be lucrative. She needed to have a way to contribute to the household. Two incomes were better than one. Ask me how I know.

"Dad, relax. Blossom is a great girl, you'll see. She has time to find a job."

"True," I mumbled.

"She speaks highly of her mother, who she said is very chill. I think the two of you will get along great." He was smiling the entire time he talked.

"You hope," I said in a clipped voice.

Manuel laughed, as if I had said something funny. "I'm not worried."

I was worried enough for the two of us.

"Want to see a picture of her?" he asked, his voice sounding hopeful.

"Oh, now you want to share pictures. Sure. Let me see what this Blossom person looks like." I suddenly realized I sounded like a cranky old man and was probably putting a damper on his excitement.

I softened my words with a faint smile, and he whipped out his phone and showed me his Instagram page.

"There she is," he said, enlarging a photo of him and a young woman sitting on a blanket in the grass. He had an arm around her, and she was resting her head on his shoulder.

I eyed him sideways and wondered if he was letting his hormones cloud his judgment.

I scrolled through a few more photos. Going strictly by these pictures, he had chosen well. She was definitely a looker, with light brown skin and her hair cut into a short, curly Afro. Her most stunning feature was her eyes. They were big and bright with long lashes. I immediately understood why my son had fallen for her, which became a reason for concern. He might be thinking with the head in his pants and not the one on his shoulders.

"You have that look on your face," Manuel said.

"What look?"

"Your skeptical look."

I paused, wondering how to express my concerns without sounding condescending. "Look, I know you're an adult, but I can't help but wonder if you're moving a little fast. You haven't known this young woman very long."

"What happened to 'when you know, you know'? You said those exact words to me once," he said.

Internally, I sighed, tabling an argument that would probably get me nowhere. "Let's try to make the best of the meeting. I'll remain impartial and give your fiancée"—I grimaced at the word—"the benefit of the doubt."

"That's all I'm asking for. I promise, once you meet her and get to know her, you'll fall in love with her too." He took back his phone. "We should be able to nail down the dinner location later today, and then I'll let Blossom know everything's a go. I'll let you get cleaned up, and then we can ride in to work together?"

"Sure."

"I'll wait for you in the living room."

I watched him walk out the door before making my way to the adjoining bathroom, shifting gears to the work I had to tackle when I went into the office.

I was currently working on a deal that had me pulling my hair out. A family with three car washes across the city had been duped into a predatory loan that was draining their profits. I was struggling to find a way to get them out of it before they lost everything.

I got into this business because I liked working with numbers and helping people achieve their dreams. I wasn't much of a risk-taker myself, so helping businesses expand gave me a sense of satisfaction and made me feel as if I were contributing to the long-term growth of my community. Finding out another banker had taken advantage of these people's naivety, which could cause them to lose everything, angered me.

"Not if I can help it," I mumbled, as I stripped out of my clothes.

As the cool water beat down on my face, I thought about my son and his engagement. When his mother and I divorced and they moved to Arizona, I was devastated. Fortunately, when he turned thirteen, he moved in with me. "To help him become a man," his mother had said, though I suspected she simply wanted him out of the way so she could start dating again.

I didn't mind. I was happy to have him back in my life and my home, and I liked to think I had done a decent job raising him to make the right choices in life.

I guess I'd find out how good of a job I'd done on Friday night when I met his fiancée.

Chapter 3

Jamison

Thanks to a cancellation at Knife & Fork, Mindy was able to get us a reservation. We arrived at the restaurant fifteen minutes early, which annoyed my son, but since I was driving, he had no choice but to come along.

I didn't like to rush and believed arriving early gave me the upper hand. With clients, it worked well, establishing right away that I was trustworthy and reliable, and it subtly gave them the impression they were stepping into an environment I controlled. In the case of Blossom and her mother, arriving early wasn't about leverage so much as preparation. I had time to settle, observe, and brace myself.

The dining room was packed, and though I hadn't been hungry before I arrived, the scent of sizzling meat and spices made my mouth water. I'd never had a bad meal here, so I was looking forward to dinner. The hostess led us to a well-appointed table toward the back, round and covered in a white tablecloth. We weren't near a window, but thankfully, we weren't in the middle of the dining room, either.

Manuel and I were browsing the menus when my son said, "There she is." His voice had taken on a hushed quality.

I followed his line of sight to the two women coming our way, and I was immediately struck by how clearly they resembled each other. Both were striking, with beautiful eyes and a confident bearing, but the similarities ended there.

Blossom was lighter, her curls cropped close to her head. Her mother, on the other hand, was several shades darker, with a chestnut-brown complexion. While Blossom's style leaned toward polished and modern, her mother's was unapologetically bohemian. She was so colorful that the rest of the room seemed gray in comparison.

Her waist-length dreadlocks were pulled back from her face with a red-and-gold scarf, the silk fabric knotted with casual precision. She wore a clay-colored blouse that was loose and flowing, the kind that skimmed rather than clung, with a modest neckline allowing several long necklaces to rest against her chest, layered and mismatched. A full skirt in vibrant colors swayed and whispered around her ankles as she walked, with flat leather sandals peeking out from beneath the hem.

I vaguely remembered Manuel mentioning she owned an herbal store and had a yoga studio, and she looked exactly like the kind of woman who did. A cloth crossbody bag patterned with oversized sunflowers hung diagonally across her torso, and bangles—too many to count—circled her wrists, chiming softly as they approached the table.

Her gaze boldly met mine, and my stomach tensed in an unusual way. I had the uncomfortable sense that, despite my early arrival, I didn't necessarily have the upper hand.

As I rose to my feet, my son rushed over to his fiancée and greeted her with a hug. I suspected if I and Blossom's mother weren't present, their greeting would have been more amorous.

Manuel slipped an arm around his fiancée, his face lighting up with a smile bigger than the one he had worn when I bought him the bike he wanted many Christmases ago.

"Dad, this is my fiancée, Blossom Nabors."

Manuel's face beamed with pride and expectation, but I saw the moment he held his breath. I hated to see him so nervous and decided I would do my best not to spoil the night for him.

I put on my most gregarious smile, the one I used when meeting clients or having to smooth over a particularly thorny deal.

"Very nice to meet you, Blossom."

She had a good, strong handshake.

Green flag.

I turned my attention to her mother and noticed the diamond stud twinkling in her left nostril. Before me was a forty-something-year-old woman dressed like a carefree twenty-year-old, right down to the ring in her nose. I was mildly intrigued.

I extended my hand. "Jamison Harris. Nice to meet you, Ms. Nabors."

The clasp of her hand wasn't particularly strong, but it was surprisingly soft. Unexpectedly, I wanted to hold onto her longer and had to remind myself to let go.

"It's Washington. I dropped my ex-husband's last name years ago, but you can call me Tallulah."

Divorced, like me, which explained why Blossom's father was living in Georgia now.

"And you can call me Jamison," I said.

I reclaimed my seat, with Manuel sitting to my right. He and Blossom leaned toward each other and started talking quietly.

Tallulah sat to my left, and she smelled amazing. I couldn't place the scent because it wasn't a combination I had smelled before. The fragrance was unique and earthy. A little bit enticing, if I were being honest.

The waiter appeared at the table, a young man with a slicked-back ponytail. "Good evening, ladies and gentlemen. Can I start you off with a drink while you decide on your dinner?" he asked with practiced enthusiasm.

"Water for me, please," Blossom said.

"Me, too," Manuel said.

"I'll take a glass of cranberry juice, no ice," Tallulah said.

Interesting choice.

I ordered a glass of red wine. When the waiter left, an uneasy silence settled over the table. Manuel and Blossom remained wrapped up in each other, leaving Tallulah and me to fill the conversational void.

I cleared my throat. "Manuel mentioned that you own an herbal store?"

"I do, but it's a little more than an herbal store. Simply Well is the name, and it's in the arts district downtown, in a building that was recently bought."

"Are you talking about the Freedom Capital Building?" I asked. My role as a commercial banker meant I stayed abreast of all the major business moves in our city.

She nodded, adjusting one of her necklaces. The pendant looked like raw rose quartz. "That's the one. My center is on the ground floor, and we offer yoga classes, reiki and reflexology, herbal consultations, and meditation workshops, that sort of thing."

"Interesting." I kept my tone neutral. I didn't want to let on that I was skeptical about alternative medicine and wellness as a viable business. "How long have you been in business?"

"Ten years this fall."

Shocking. The industry seemed oversaturated, the margins were slim, and startups had a high failure rate. "Impressive. Congratulations."

"Thank you." There was a slight edge to her voice, as if she'd heard the surprise in mine and didn't appreciate it. "I love the work I do and have managed to find loyal, regular customers."

Blossom glanced up from her menu. "Mom's being modest. Her workshops always sell out within days, and she has a great reputation in the community, which is why she has so many repeat customers. People trust her and know she's not one of those fakes offering generic solutions that don't work."

Tallulah waved a hand dismissively, her bangles knocking against each other like wind chimes. "She's making me sound much grander than I am."

"Doubtful," I said thoughtfully. "Your business has survived a decade in a tough industry. You must be doing something right."

She smiled briefly at the compliment. "You're in banking, is that right?"

"Commercial banking. In a nutshell, I finance deals for businesses of all sizes."

"Sounds..." She paused, searching for the right word. "Rigid."

Was that a compliment or an insult?

"It can be," I admitted. "Though we're allowed to color outside the lines on occasion. Helping a business owner secure the right financing solution is very satisfying work."

"I'm sure it is, but in all honesty, numbers and spreadsheets have never been my strong suit. I do what I have to and leave the rest to my accountant." She let out a little laugh, but her dark eyes studied me with curious intensity.

"What do you consider your strength?" I asked.

"My intuition. Being able to trust my gut and go with the flow, to see which direction the universe guides me in. It's the reason I took a leap of faith and opened my wellness center, despite the people closest to me trying to talk me out of it."

"I see," I said, though I didn't see at all.

I was a planner and analyzed problems from all angles to find solutions and determine how to proceed. Going with the flow had never been part of my vocabulary, and I'd never once relied on the universe to guide my steps. I didn't even know what that meant.

Tallulah seemed nice enough, but I was beginning to suspect she was too woo-woo for my taste. If Blossom was anything like her, I had concerns because I'd raised Manuel to be sensible and practical.

"Different people have different approaches," I added.

The waiter returned, placing our beverages beside us. "Ready to order?" he asked.

"Order anything you like. Dinner is on me," I announced to the table.

My son shot an appreciative smile in my direction.

Tallulah lifted her gaze from her menu, surprise on her face. "You don't have to do that."

"I insist. After all, we're about to be family."

"That's very generous of you."

"May I have two more minutes?" Blossom asked.

"Sure. I'll be back in a little bit." The waiter left again.

I relaxed into my chair. As far as I was concerned, the night was off to a good start. My son was the most important person in the world to me, and if he loved this young lady, I wanted to make sure she was comfortable joining our family despite her mother's unconventional style of decision-making.

I still wasn't completely on board with my son getting

married so soon out of college to a young woman he'd only known a short time. But tonight could be a successful meeting of the families.

I would do my part to make that happen.

Chapter 4

Tallulah

I already knew what I wanted for dinner because I had reviewed the menu ahead of time, but my eyes skimmed the choices to reconfirm I wanted the salmon salad.

Though studying the menu, I was oddly conscious of the man to my right. Was he good-looking? Yes. But not in a drop-dead gorgeous, head-turning way. In a polished, respectable way. The Caucasian version of my ex-husband.

He had a headful of glossy dark brown hair, cut low and graying at the temples. Faint lines had settled at the corners of his eyes, which appeared as captivating pools of light gray. His lips weren't particularly remarkable—somewhere between thin and full—but his jawline... well, that was remarkably square. Perhaps Jamison's best feature. I wouldn't be surprised if his jawline could cut through concrete.

He wore a navy-blue suit and a dark tie. A very conservative appearance compared to his son, whose tan jacket and red tie seemed more relaxed and complemented his darker complexion. They'd both clearly come right from work.

At first glance, I had assumed that if Jamison smiled, his

face would crack. Instead, the initial smile softened his features and made him seem more approachable, but I could definitely see the rigidity in him that Blossom had mentioned.

Most of the time, the only meat I ate was seafood, with the occasional chicken thrown in. When I didn't feel like eating either of those, a big bowl of vegetables was my go-to. The menu had an interesting vegetarian option, but I idly considered ordering the lobster. Such a decision would definitely not make a good impression on Jamison and embarrass my daughter. But boy, was I tempted. I hadn't had lobster in a long time, and I'm sure a restaurant like this made a great dish. Jamison did say to get anything you want, didn't he?

I knew he didn't mean get *anything* you want. No one ever meant those words when they said them. What they really meant was, get anything you want within reason. I closed the menu.

"You've made a decision?" Jamison asked.

I nodded. "I'm going to have the salmon salad."

"Salmon salad?"

He sounded appalled. Downright disappointed. Maybe I should have ordered the lobster.

"They have great steaks. I bring clients here at least twice a month," he continued.

"Mom doesn't eat red meat," Blossom volunteered.

"What a surprise," Jamison said.

Did I hear sarcasm? His response sounded like sarcasm, as if a detail he already suspected had been confirmed.

Now he was looking at me as if I were a being from another planet. Guessing the question coming next, I answered before he asked.

"I didn't give up red meat for religious reasons or because I have any ethical concerns about those animals—though that's a conversation we should be having. It's purely for health reasons. I cut out red meat and processed meat years ago because they've been linked to a greater increase in heart disease, are carcinogenic to humans, and cause inflammation, which creates all kinds of problems in the body. Food is medicine, as they say, and I take that very seriously."

"She's very conscientious about what she puts into her body," Blossom said.

I smiled at her. "I'm not as good as I should be, but I try to do my part."

"Too much of anything is bad for you, isn't it?" Jamison sipped his wine.

"Sure. But too much of certain things is worse," I said.

He mulled my statement for a while. "Is red meat the only food you won't eat?"

"I eliminated pork a while back, so mostly I eat seafood and all sorts of fruits and vegetables."

"You're pescatarian," Manuel said.

"Not really. I enjoy an occasional piece of chicken, and I always have turkey at Thanksgiving," I said with a laugh. "But for the most part, yes."

The waiter returned, placing a basket of warm bread in the middle of the table and then taking our orders. Jamison ordered the ribeye, medium-rare. Absolutely unsurprising considering how he praised the steaks here. I went with the salmon salad, as planned, while Manuel and Blossom also ordered steaks and asked for wine with their meals.

They seemed to be in tune with each other. Both ordered waters to start. Both ordered steaks and wine with their meals.

Jamison took a piece of bread and passed the basket around the table. By the time our food arrived, conversation was flowing easily as we got to know each other.

"How did you two meet? Blossom mentioned something

about food trucks, but I don't know the details." I ate some of my yummy salmon.

The kids put down their forks and looked at each other.

"Do you want to tell the story?" Blossom asked.

"You start. I'll jump in if you say anything wrong," Manuel teased.

Blossom laughed, as if he were a stand-up comedian delivering the best line of the night.

"Okay, so there was a food truck rally near campus, and a few of my friends and I decided to go—to eat something different from the usual dreck they gave us on campus." She wrinkled her nose.

Blossom made it sound as if they didn't have good choices. There were literal chain restaurants on campus, giving them delicious options in addition to the food offered in the dining halls, which were also very good. Dreck? I could tell her about dreck. That's what we were served when I was a college student, and we certainly didn't have as many amenities. I'll never forget jealously touring the campus with her and seriously considering re-enrolling because of all the improvements.

"Everyone who knows me knows I love a good taco, so of course I made a beeline for the taco truck," Blossom continued.

"I saw her in line," Manuel continued, his eyes on my daughter. "I was over at the pizza truck and couldn't take my eyes off her."

Blossom blushed. Okay, they were cute.

"I had to meet her, so I left my line and went to the taco truck."

"Even though he wanted pizza!" Blossom exclaimed, throwing up her hands. She often spoke with her hands, which was amusing to watch.

"I no longer cared about pizza." Manuel shrugged. "After

working up the nerve, I struck up a conversation with her and asked about the menu."

"As if he couldn't read," Blossom said.

"I needed an excuse to talk to you," he admitted.

Jamison sipped his wine. I wasn't looking directly at him, so I couldn't read his expression. I wondered if he was enjoying this cute story as much as I was.

"We kept talking until it was my turn to order, which I did. He didn't order anything but asked if I'd like to keep talking. I said yes," Blossom said coyly.

"I knew then that I had her," Manuel gloated, gesturing as if he'd cast out a line and was reeling in a fish.

Blossom bumped him with her shoulder, and they both laughed.

"Then what happened?" Jamison asked.

"Then she stood in line with me at the pizza truck. After I paid for my meal, we sat down on the grass together and continued talking."

"What happened to your friends?" I asked.

"They saw us but left us alone. At least my guy friends did." Manuel laughed.

"My friends texted a couple of times until I told them I was fine, and if they wanted to leave, they could go back to campus without me," Blossom added.

"We must have stayed there what... three hours?" Manuel asked.

"At least," Blossom agreed. "Finally, we walked back to campus and exchanged numbers. We've been together ever since."

"That's a lovely story. You met in February, about four months ago, correct?" I knew the answer but had purposely supplied the information for Jamison's benefit, in case he didn't know.

Manuel's face suddenly became serious. "I know the timeline seems like we're rushing, but I've never felt this way about anyone but your daughter, Ms. Washington."

"Young love does have a tendency to be impatient," Jamison observed.

"Dad, we're not that young," Manuel said with a hint of exasperation. "We're both twenty-two years old. We're college graduates. We know who we are and what we want."

Though I couldn't see their hands, I could tell the moment he reached for Blossom under the table.

"We've talked about everything you could imagine," my daughter added. "We've discussed our career goals, what part of town we want to live in, kids. Everything. We're on the same page about all of it."

Jamison and I exchanged glances. Though we were basically strangers, for a brief moment, we shared the same concern: that our kids might be moving too fast, and there was nothing we could do to slow them down. They were in love and determined to move forward. They also clearly wanted our blessing.

"Congratulations on finding your other half in this crazy world," I said. "I'm here if you need me for anything. Advice. Venting. The offer includes you too, Manuel. But not too much on my daughter, okay?"

He laughed. "Yes, ma'am."

"Same goes for me. I'm here if you need me." Jamison raised his glass. "To our children, Manuel and Blossom. I wish you nothing but the best."

I lifted my half-full glass of cranberry juice. "So do I. I know you probably haven't thought this far ahead, but my first piece of advice is to suggest a spring wedding under a new moon. In spring, your energy aligns with growth and renewal, while marrying under a new moon is perfect for new beginnings and building a lasting life together." Had I taken my own advice, my marriage might have lasted.

Jamison turned his head in my direction, but I ignored him because I noticed the smiles on Blossom and Manuel's faces had faltered.

"Is something wrong?" I asked.

They didn't *have* to get married in the spring under a new moon. I was only making a suggestion. Maybe I shouldn't have brought up my beliefs. I'd probably embarrassed Blossom and confused Manuel.

"No. We, uh..." My daughter glanced at her fiancé.

"We've already picked a date," Manuel said.

"I didn't know you had already decided on a date. What date did you pick?" Jamison asked.

"We're getting married on September twentieth. In three months."

Jamison and I slowly lowered our glasses at the same time.

"Three months!" we exclaimed.

Chapter 5

Tallulah

Jamison waved over the waiter.

"Yes, sir?"

"I'm gonna need more wine."

"Yes, sir."

As he walked away, I turned my attention to Manuel and my daughter. "September twentieth is an ambitious timeline. Why the rush?" I asked.

"We're in love. We figured, why wait?" Blossom shot a glance at Manuel.

They had no idea what they were getting themselves into. I had been overwhelmed by the complications of my wedding and its planning, even though Karl and I were engaged for over a year. Three months was not enough time unless Blossom and Manuel weren't planning a formal affair.

"Are you doing something small, like going to the courthouse?" I asked.

They both laughed, as if my suggestion was completely ridiculous.

"We want to have a regular wedding with friends and family celebrating with us," Blossom replied.

"Then you need time to plan. You have to find a venue, shop for a dress, plan the menu, send out invitations. There's so much to do, Blossom."

"We know, and we'll accelerate our timeline."

She spoke in a reasonable voice. So young. So idealistic.

"How do you plan to pay for this wedding in three months?" Jamison interjected.

Manuel responded this time. "I'm going to use the money in my brokerage account."

"Like hell you are!" Jamison said in a low, vehement voice.

Manuel's cheeks reddened. "It's my money."

"For your future," his father countered.

"Blossom is my future." Manuel's lips firmed.

Though he wasn't thinking clearly, his reply was very romantic. Jamison clearly didn't agree, because his lips flattened in annoyance.

"Weddings are expensive, and the budget would eat through the money in your account," he pointed out.

"I have plenty, and I won't use it all. Getting married is an important event. Blossom and I want to have the type of wedding that we want, but we're going to be very thoughtful about the budget."

Jamison leaned across the table. "Marriage is more than warm fuzzies and vibes. It's responsibility. It's work. It's a fifty-fifty partnership—"

I let out an involuntary laugh. To cover, I immediately shoved a morsel of salmon in my mouth.

Jamison glared at me. "Did I say something funny?"

I considered ignoring him or lying and acting as if what he had said was not the reason for my laughter. Then I changed my mind.

"What part of marriage is fifty-fifty, and how do you keep score?"

He appeared annoyed, shifting in his chair to face me fully. "No one is keeping score, but each party should be able to contribute financially."

A loaded comment if I ever heard one. I had no doubt he was talking about my daughter because she didn't have a job yet.

"Dad!" Manuel exclaimed.

I sat up to my full height, turning to face Jamison too. "There is more to marriage than the financial aspects, and *each party* can contribute in different ways, such as caretaking, cooking—"

"The top two reasons for divorce are cheating and financial problems, so I think my opinion trumps yours, and right now we're talking about money."

"How much money is enough?" I asked. "Marriage is not a business transaction. It should be about love and compatibility, but I guess you don't understand that because it doesn't fit on a spreadsheet."

"Mom, please!" Blossom hissed.

I heard my daughter but ignored her, having flashbacks to similar arguments with her father about money and structure and the way he prioritized them in our marriage. Manuel seemed more level-headed than his stuck-up, rigid father, but I was concerned Jamison could exert influence over him, to the detriment of my daughter.

No way in hell was I letting her marry into *this* family. I did not want her to go through the same crap I had to deal with while married to her father.

"I understand plenty about marriage, Ms. Washington, and I understand that love doesn't pay the mortgage. Compatibility doesn't keep the lights on. When things get tough—and they will—a couple needs a solid foundation, which means stability and both parties pulling their own weight."

What an insufferable pig!

"Pulling their own weight?" I repeated, my voice going up an octave. "What does that mean, exactly, *Mister* Harris? Earning enough money to meet whatever arbitrary standards you've outlined? Because I'm starting to think you don't believe my daughter is good enough for your son simply because she hasn't found a job yet."

"I never said—"

"You didn't have to! It's written all over your smug face." I gestured at his head, my bracelets crashing against each other with the movement. "I'm sure you've been calculating her worth all night, trying to determine if you should plug her into the liability or asset column."

I watched with satisfaction as his square jaw tightened and anger infused his cheeks with color. "*Not* true. I'm simply being realistic, instead of putting my trust in moonbeams and fairy dust."

I inhaled sharply at the jab.

"I have sacrificed to make sure my son has a better life than I do, and he has done his part by working hard and building his savings. He has a career path and goals, and I want to make sure he continues making smart decisions."

"Marrying my daughter isn't making a smart decision?"

"That's not what I—"

"I'm sure he worked very hard to get a job at the same bank where his father works. Too bad I don't have any strings I can pull to ensure my daughter gets a job right out of college." My comment was bitchy, but he asked for it.

Blossom gasped. "Mom!"

"Dad, enough!"

I leaned forward, holding Jamison's gray gaze and lowering

my voice to avoid yelling and embarrassing us all in this fine establishment. "Stop measuring their relationship based on dollars and cents. What actually matters in a marriage is not how it looks on paper."

"What matters," Jamison said, his voice dangerously calm as he also leaned forward, "is whether they can build a life together in the real world. Not a fantasy world fueled by positive energy and going with the flow."

The second jab landed.

"So if the benefits can't be quantified on a profit and loss statement, they're no good?"

He sighed, shaking his head as if speaking to a difficult toddler. "You have to be realistic, Ms. Washington. We, all four of us, need to be smart about what these two young people are getting themselves into. Rushing into marriage because it feels good is a recipe for disaster."

I sat back, arms folded over my chest. Unbelievable. I had my concerns about Blossom and Manuel rushing into marriage, but Jamison's beliefs were way off. He was concerned about money. I wanted to ensure their energies were aligned so they wouldn't be making a mistake. As long as they loved each other and were properly aligned, everything should work out.

"Sometimes you have to take a leap of faith and believe in the connection you have."

"A leap of faith ends in disaster without a solid financial foundation. This is a statistical fact. I'm not making this up. Financial incompatibility is a problem and shouldn't be ignored in favor of romance and butterflies in your stomach."

"Is that what happened to you?" I asked.

His expression shuttered. "Our conversation is about Blossom and Manuel."

"I don't know, sounds like you're projecting the mistakes from your failed marriage onto our children."

He chuckled, and despite knowing it wasn't a real laugh, I couldn't help but notice how much more handsome he looked when the scowl on his face was replaced by a smile. And why did my heart make an odd little leap, as if an electrical spark had shot through the muscle? As if I enjoyed the sound of his amusement?

"You've got some nerve accusing me of projecting when it's obvious you're projecting. You're determined to prove none of the practical aspects of a relationship matter because... let me guess... you had all the practical matters attended to when you married, but the chakra was off. Am I right?"

"Not once did I use the word chakra, you ass."

He flung his hands in the air. "Oh, now I'm an ass. You want to see an ass? Check the mirror, lady."

I shot to my feet, my chair scraping the floor. "I'm so glad we had the opportunity to meet. My daughter deserves better than to marry into a family that considers her a financial risk."

He muttered a curse under his breath, but I heard the f-bomb loud and clear. I'm not entirely certain he didn't want me to hear it.

"No one said—"

"You didn't have to." I snatched up my purse. "My daughter is smart, capable, funny, charming, loving, and on her way to great things. Her lack of current employment doesn't make her unworthy of your son."

"I never said she was unworthy." Jamison's eyes flashed as he looked up at me.

"You implied it with your fifty-fifty comment and your concerns about Manuel's savings account." I turned to my daughter. "Blossom, we're leaving. Let's go."

Her eyes widened with mortification. "Mom, I can't—"

"Let's. Go."

Right then, the server returned with Jamison's wine.

"Thank you." He took the glass before the server could place it on the table and gulped a mouthful as if it were hard liquor.

"Ma'am, is there something I can help you with?" the server asked, looking confused because I was standing at the table.

"I'm fine, but I'll be leaving shortly. Could you give us a moment, please?"

"Of course." He backed away and went to tend to one of his other tables.

Manuel stood abruptly. "Ms. Washington—"

I lifted my hand. "It was very nice to meet you, Manuel." I swung my gaze to his father. "You, not so much."

Jamison narrowed his eyes, opened his mouth to say something, and then closed it immediately. He then started eating his steak.

Asshole.

"Blossom. Let's. Go."

My daughter stood slowly, head bent.

Manuel briefly grabbed her wrist. "I'll call you," he said.

She nodded and meekly followed me out of the restaurant.

Chapter 6

Tallulah

I might have overreacted.

Though I was still fuming, I was thinking more clearly as Blossom and I sat in the back of the Lyft.

Perhaps I could have tempered my words a little, but it was difficult when someone was taking jabs at my kid. Jamison Harris had to be the most aggravating man I had ever met. That's really saying something, considering I was married to Karl Nabors, the previous reigning Champ of Aggravating Men.

I should have kept my cool, but the minute he made loaded comments about money, all I saw was red as I went back in time to life with Blossom's father. A man who tossed around the words "frugal" and "prudent" but was really a cheapskate and a tightwad, as tightly wound as a watch spring.

He loved rubbing it in my face that he was able to pay for Blossom's college education because he'd planned and saved, as if I hadn't contributed at all to her life or education. His condescension burned. And hurt. Like when we were married, and he belittled my contributions to the household as a mother and homemaker. Then, when Blossom started school, I got a part-time job, and he referred to it as my "little gig." Though his snark dampened my spirits, I was proud of myself and happy I no longer had to go to him for money.

"Are you going to stay mad at me all night?" I whispered so the driver couldn't hear.

Blossom sat with her arms crossed over her chest, staring straight ahead. Her emotions had gone from sad to angry, and as a result, she hadn't said two words to me since we climbed into the back seat of this car.

I sighed loudly. "I'm sorry."

"I asked you to do me *one* favor, and you couldn't. The entire night was ruined! Why do you have to be so dramatic about everything?" Blossom demanded.

Her words hurt. "The night wasn't ruined by me," I said defensively.

"Manuel's father hates us now, and he probably won't let him marry me."

Now who's being dramatic? I thought. "I seriously doubt that will happen."

She twisted sideways in the seat, her eyes boring into mine. "Manuel respects his father's opinion." With a jerky movement, she turned to stare straight ahead again.

I didn't want her to be upset, but calling off the wedding might not be a bad idea. At least postponing it for a while. Jamison and I agreed on one thing—the kids might be rushing—though we had different reasons for our beliefs.

After meeting Jamison, I wasn't so sure I liked the idea of my daughter having him as a father-in-law. It wasn't her fault she was struggling to find work. I could practically see the judgment leaking out of that man's pores, but she had sent out at least two dozen resumes and had applied for positions she was clearly overqualified for. Sadly, she'd had a few interviews but no callbacks.

We didn't talk anymore on the ride home. When we arrived at the house, we silently walked up the steps to the covered front porch, and the lights automatically came on.

Inside, Blossom went in the direction of her bedroom.

Our home was a modest three-bedroom, two-bath house, decorated in an eclectic style that made it feel warm and cozy. Soft, woven throws were tossed over the backs of chairs, and rugs in bright colors adorned the hardwood floors.

I never met a decorative pillow I didn't like, and there were plenty in varying fabrics on the furniture, with a group of large ones stacked high on the floor, corralled by an oversized woven basket. On nights when the house was filled with guests, they doubled as floor seating, turning the living room into a casual gathering space.

My furniture was a mix of old and new, far from pristine or high-end. The color palette included warm creams and sandy beiges accented by terracotta, deep olive, and the occasional burst of turquoise. During the day, light poured in through the huge windows, dousing my plants with much-needed sunshine.

As I strolled into the kitchen, I remembered why I fell in love with this house. It was a Craftsman bungalow and reminded me of similar houses popular in certain neighborhoods in Atlanta. It wasn't 'cookie-cutter' like so many of the homes Karl and I had looked at when we were house-hunting. It had history and character.

My ex-husband liked it because it was a foreclosure, so we got it for a steal. Well, he got it for a steal. I was pregnant and not working then. I would have followed him anywhere, and did, leaving my job and the comfort of my extended family in Georgia to move to the Midwest with him, where his family was located.

Not long after we divorced, he returned to Georgia with his new wife to be near her aging parents, leaving me and Blossom behind. His family... well, they weren't so helpful once he was gone. They loved Blossom but tolerated me and had always referred to me as "weird."

I was used to it, but the way they distanced themselves from my daughter after his departure had been painfully disappointing. I considered moving back to Georgia but hadn't wanted to disrupt Blossom's schooling and take her away from her friends.

So we stayed. Then my business took off, and moving became less attractive.

I took a wellness shot from the refrigerator and tossed it back, grimacing as the ginger burned the back of my throat. In the pantry, I removed a mason jar filled with my homemade granola and popped a handful in my mouth.

Blossom and I needed to talk. The energy in the house was off, making the air tight and unsettled because she was upset with me. I couldn't bring myself to go to bed without smoothing things over, something Karl and I should have done more often. Maybe if we had faced our problems instead of letting them harden into silence, we would still be married. Instead, he had dismissed my beliefs about energy and intention, and eventually, I had stopped sharing them.

Taking my snack with me, I went down the hall to Blossom's bedroom and knocked on the door.

"Yes?" she answered.

"Can I come in?"

There was a pause, and for a second I thought she'd say no. Then the door swung open. She looked at me briefly and then walked away, dropping onto the edge of the bed.

I handed her the granola.

"I'm upset. You can't bribe me with your delicious granola, Mom." She poured some into her hand.

"I know. I didn't come in here to bribe you. I came to talk."

I took back the jar and sat across from her in the rolling chair by her desk. "I know tonight didn't go as planned, and I apologize for my part in ruining the evening. In my defense, I didn't appreciate Manuel's father insinuating you weren't good enough for his son."

"I'm sure he didn't appreciate you insinuating his son only got his job because of his father. Manuel is really smart, Mom. He had to go through three rounds of interviews and then waited several weeks in limbo, not knowing if he'd gotten the position. His biggest concern was screwing up and embarrassing his father after he had stuck his neck out for him. Yes, Mr. Harris got Manuel's foot in the door, but he earned his position because he knows his stuff."

"I'm sure he does," I said.

We both ate some granola.

"Manuel isn't like his dad," Blossom said in a low voice.

I was horrified to see tears shimmering in her eyes. "My love..."

"I know you want to protect me, but you don't have to protect me from Manuel. He's not going to hurt me. He loves me as much as I love him, and I don't want to lose him, Mom." Her voice thickened.

I didn't know what to say.

"Would you talk to Mr. Harris?" Blossom asked tentatively.

"Talk to him? About what?"

"Tell him you didn't mean what you said tonight."

"You want me to lie?"

"*Mom.*"

I pressed my fingers to my temple. "Slow down for a minute, and let me think."

My daughter's eyes, so much like mine, filled with hope. I had meant what I said, and now she wanted me to retract my words. My insides tightened, rejecting what she wanted me to do. Why couldn't Jamison retract his words? Or why couldn't we agree to disagree?

I was at the age where I didn't feel the need to mince words, and I certainly didn't want to pretend what I said wasn't true. I had learned over the years that honesty and being direct was best.

"I, uh . . ." I hesitated.

"Please. I'm begging you." Her eyes pleaded with me.

I didn't really care what Jamison Harris thought, but I loved my daughter more than life, and her opinion mattered to me. Her happiness mattered to me, and right now she wasn't happy.

"Okay, I'll talk to him, but after the weekend. We both need time to calm down. I'll reach out to him next week, but I'm not making any promises because our conversation might not go well."

"Thank you," Blossom said in a relieved voice.

She seemed genuinely distraught that Jamison would convince his son not to marry her. Clearly, my daughter was madly in love with this young man, but did he love her? Would he be careful with my baby's heart?

"Three months, huh?"

She nodded, a smile breaking out on her face.

"Doesn't give us much time to plan a wedding," I said.

"I know, but we don't want to wait."

"Assuming the conversation between Manuel's father and I goes well, we need to start planning, figuring out a budget—all the things."

Perking up, she nodded vigorously.

"By the way, Manuel is not paying for everything."

"But he said—"

"I don't care what he said. Were you at Knife & Fork tonight? Did you hear what his father said?"

Her shoulders slumped. "I don't have any money. How can I contribute?"

"Your father and I will contribute on your behalf." I didn't have any qualms about suggesting Karl help with the wedding expenses. Despite having two more children with his new wife, he never forgot about Blossom or treated her differently. He simply never hesitated to dote on his firstborn.

"You don't have a lot of money, Mom."

"I have *some* money. It's not a lot, but I want to help. It's not every day my only child gets married."

She smiled.

"I'll take care of the cake, and once you've figured out a budget, I'll see what else I can cover."

"You're sure?" she asked.

"Positive. Are we good?"

"Yeah, we're good. Thank you, Mom."

I rose from the chair. "Wonderful. Sleep tight. I'll see you in the morning."

Before heading to bed, I lit a bundle of sage and moved slowly through the living room, then the hallway, letting the smoke curl into the corners where tension liked to linger. I paused outside Blossom's bedroom door longer than I did the rest of the house, whispering a silent intention for calm and clarity before moving on.

The ritual didn't erase conflict, but it helped me mentally release what I couldn't fix in one night, removing the negative energy from the house and allowing me to sleep peacefully once I climbed into bed.

Chapter 7

Tallulah

The door to my store opened, and I turned from rearranging my organic teas on one of the shelves. Mrs. Chen from the Far East Market next door walked in.

"Hello, Tallulah," she said with a little wave, strolling over.

Mrs. Chen was almost eighty years old, but if not for her gray hairs, you wouldn't know it. She was very agile, walking around the building several times a day as a form of exercise. She also did Tai Chi in the park on Saturdays with a group of Chinese women. I had tried more than once to convince her to teach classes for me, but she had always declined.

Her eyes crinkled in the corners as she surveyed the shelves I had been working on. She rested her hands on her hips. "Moving things around again? When will you be satisfied?" she asked.

I laughed at her teasing. "When I die," I said.

She tutted. "Do not talk like that. I saw a lot of people with their yoga mats today. Julie must have a full class."

Julie was a yoga instructor who rented space from me and

conducted classes Monday through Saturday. Behind a half wall at the back of the store was a hallway leading to a quieter part of the center. The yoga studio occupied the largest room in the back, with bamboo floors, a mirrored wall, and dimmed lights. She taught a couple of classes during the day, and one after the shop closed. Two smaller rooms located farther down the hall were also rented. One for massage therapy and the other for treatments like reiki and reflexology.

"Almost," I replied. "Wednesdays are becoming popular, it seems. I think people are stressed and need a midweek break."

Mrs. Chen hummed her agreement. "I can understand that."

After years of knowing each other, we didn't need to talk all the time and fell into an easy silence while she browsed the supplements, and I continued rearranging the teas. We'd had plenty of long conversations over the years and occasionally ate lunch together—either in my store or hers.

My wellness center wasn't big and fancy, but I was proud of it. I hadn't always wanted to be a business owner, but running the store combined my desire to help others with the ability to earn a living. I was proud of my little spot, and every inch of space was carefully used. The calming, clean scent of citrus and ginger from infused oils filled the air, and the small refrigerator hummed quietly near the counter, filled with my latest kombucha inventory.

Yoga mats stood upright in a wicker basket near books on mindfulness and proper nutrition. My essential oils collection was vast, as were my natural skincare products and herbal supplements. A small table showcased healing crystals. I didn't sell many, but I liked to keep them on hand for customers who needed them. My bestsellers were rose quartz for balance and calm—a personal favorite of mine—lapis lazuli for inner strength, and citrine for confidence and success.

Healthy snacks occupied a rack in one corner: trail mixes, protein bars, dark chocolate sweetened with dates. I also stacked them on the counter for impulse purchases. When Blossom used to work in the store with me, she'd sneak some of the chocolate or the trail mix with chocolate pieces. Hard to believe those days were long gone and my only child was getting married.

Married!

Mrs. Chen turned her attention to me, tilting her head slightly. "Why did you sigh?"

"I sighed?"

"Yes. Something is on your mind."

I straightened a box of ginger root tea and this time consciously released a sigh. "Blossom got engaged last week."

Mrs. Chen's face lit up. "That is wonderful news! Congratulations!" The smile faded from her face. "You are not happy."

"The engagement was a surprise."

"Oh."

"I met her fiancé for the first time on Friday night."

Mrs. Chen raised a surprised eyebrow.

"No ring," I continued. "Just—" I waved a hand vaguely "—impulse and romance and youth."

She chuckled. "Very modern. Sounds like something my grandchildren would do."

"We met the fiancé and his father for dinner, and it was a mess. His name is Manuel, his father's name is Jamison—and he's as stuffy as his name implies," I added.

Mrs. Chen's smile softened. "How bad was the mess?"

"Catastrophic." I pressed my lips together. "The father is insufferably rude, a complete square, and a tightwad. He's as bad as my ex-husband, maybe worse."

I told her everything, from the time Blossom dropped the unexpected invitation on me to the dinner that started a bit awkwardly before progressing along fine and then ending like a volcanic eruption. I was honest about my role in the blow-up.

I ended with another sigh, this one louder and longer. "My daughter wants me to apologize to him."

I had intended to contact Jamison yesterday, but I'd been busy most of the day, and since last night was the final class in my meditation series until the fall, I had stayed late to talk to students who needed additional help.

Mrs. Chen cocked her head. "She wants you to apologize to the father?"

"Yes. To Jamison."

Mrs. Chen nodded slowly. "Pride is a heavy burden to carry. Very tiring."

I let out a humorless laugh. "You don't have to tell me."

She straightened a box of oolong tea. "We have a saying." She said some words in Chinese, her voice solemn and even-toned before she translated them. "Harmony is precious. If a family lives in harmony, all affairs will prosper."

Her words settled in my chest. Basically, peace was more important than being right. Mrs. Chen often doled out advice in the same way—in a soft voice, gently, referencing some ancient Chinese saying. I had no idea if what she told me were truly Chinese proverbs, but she always made sense.

"You're right," I said.

She squeezed my hand. "The situation will improve. Blossom is a good girl. She is smart. You raised her well."

A lump appeared in my throat. My biggest worry was that I'd somehow screwed up my kid. I knew my belief system and lifestyle were odd to many people, and I'd made my share of mistakes in life. The last thing I wanted to do was raise a human who turned out to be a mess.

"Thank you. You're very kind."

"I am not being kind. I am telling you the truth. You—"

The front door opened, and in strolled Jamison Harris. I blinked, surprised. He caught sight of me and walked over, looking handsomely dapper. My body tensed with awareness.

No smile on his face, so I didn't smile either.

"Ms. Washington," he greeted in a neutral tone.

I didn't bother to remind him to call me Tallulah. "Jamison, what are you doing here?"

"Do you have a moment to talk—in private?" He smiled politely at Mrs. Chen.

She smiled back. "I was about to leave. We can continue our conversation later," she said with a meaningful look expertly hidden from Jamison's eyes.

After she was gone, I went to stand behind the front counter. For some reason, I needed a barrier between me and Jamison. "How can I help you?" I asked.

He stood ramrod straight, feet shoulder-width apart as if he owned the place. He wasn't wearing a jacket today. He wore a fitted vest and a long-sleeve white shirt that hinted at his biceps. He must work out regularly. I had underestimated his fitness during our first meeting.

"I'm here because of my son."

"Oh?"

I watched the rise and fall of his chest as he inhaled and released a quiet breath. "Manuel and I had an interesting conversation a couple of nights ago."

"I'm sure it was similar to the conversation Blossom and I had on Friday," I remarked.

Our expressions remained impassive, but I sensed a moment of understanding between us.

He cleared his throat. "My son was unhappy with me. He pointed out some... errors in my behavior. I stopped by because I don't want you to judge him based on my actions."

"I don't. Manuel seems like a lovely young man."

"He is. The best." His face softened for a fraction of a second, revealing the love and admiration he held for his child. "He's also crazy about Blossom. Madly in love with her."

"Blossom is crazy about him," I admitted.

He picked up the pen from the small cup on the counter, which customers used to sign credit card receipts. "I guess we could try to get along while the kids are making their wedding plans."

Jamison started doing the most annoying thing ever. He started clicking the pen. Again. And again. *And again.*

Annoyed, I fisted my hand under the counter. "I've been told I can get along with anyone."

He raised an eyebrow as if he doubted me, and I bit the inside of my cheek instead of making the smart remark on the tip of my tongue.

"Anything else?" I asked, keeping my voice polite. He was still clicking that damn pen.

He cleared his throat again, the clicking going faster. I briefly dropped my eyes to the pen. *What was his problem?*

"I'm sorry." The words fell from his lips as a grumble.

"Excuse me?" Did I hear him right?

"I. Am. Sorry."

I experienced an immense sense of satisfaction. So much so, I smiled. "Thank you."

His eyes narrowed slightly. "Would you like to say anything to me?"

Oh, how the mighty have fallen. This entire situation was deliciously funny. I considered letting him stew a little longer, perhaps not apologizing at all. But then I remembered my daughter's folded arms and unhappiness in the car. I remembered her plea that I make peace with her fiancé's father.

"I'm sorry too," I muttered. I wasn't used to saying those words. I barely got them out.

As if he sensed my distress, the scowl on Jamison's face shifted into a faint smile. He then returned the pen to the cup on the counter. *Thank God.* I thought I'd have to snatch it from his hand, which wouldn't help our relationship.

"Well then, I guess we're done here?" he said.

"I guess so."

He paused. "Anything for our kids, right?"

Another moment of understanding.

"Right," I agreed.

He didn't move, a thoughtful frown creasing his forehead. "Do you think they're rushing?"

"Do you?" I countered.

Neither of us wanted to come right out and say it, but we were obviously having the same doubts.

"Blossom seems like a nice young woman. I'm just..."

"I've shared my concerns with Blossom, which is all I can do. She's an adult. Manuel is an adult."

"They're adults, but adults make mistakes too."

Was he thinking about his failed marriage?

"We can offer advice all day, but we can't make them act on the advice. All we can do is provide support if they need it," I said.

He pursed his lips, then gave a single nod of agreement. "I'll let Manuel know we talked."

"And I'll do the same with Blossom."

"All right, then. See you... whenever."

Hopefully not until the rehearsal dinner, I thought.

Chapter 8

Tallulah

More than a week had passed since Jamison came by my store, and my relationship with Blossom had improved. When I went home after my conversation with Jamison, she met me at the door and gave me a big hug, exclaiming, "Thank you, Mom!"

It took me a moment to understand why she was so happy. Apparently, before I arrived at home, Manuel had called and let her know Jamison had stopped by my store and, in her words, we were friends now.

No comment.

Today, she and I were going dress shopping, and her cousin, Keke, was meeting us at the store. We had a tight window since Blossom was getting married in less than three months, but the boutique we were going to had a reputation for performing miracles.

Blossom's father had agreed to pay for her dress and had given her a generous budget to work with. All we had to do was find the perfect gown.

Today I was driving Orange Julius, my vintage Volkswagen

bus. After we finished dress shopping, I was going to drop off a few boxes I had in the back before we went to lunch. Years ago, I'd converted it into an environmentally friendly vehicle. The original internal combustion engine had been removed and replaced with an electric motor and battery, along with a complete interior overhaul. The vehicle originally belonged to my parents, and they had taken out the back rows of seats years ago, but I'd had the front and second rows reupholstered in crisp white leather, and the dashboard and gearshift updated.

My ex-husband had thought it was a waste of money to redo the old bus, but I had a deep attachment to it and couldn't let it go. Every summer, from the age of thirteen until I graduated high school, my parents took my brother and me on the road, and we traveled the country in this beautiful orange and silver bus. Because of those road trips, I had visited all 48 contiguous United States and had fond memories of the places I had seen and the people I had met.

I pulled into the plaza where the boutique was located. "We haven't talked about what kind of dress you want to buy. Do you have an idea?" I asked Blossom.

"I'm not sure. I like a few dresses that I saw with an A-line skirt, but I also like the mermaid design. Maybe something backless? I know for sure I don't want the ballgown look. Too big." She wrinkled her nose. "I'll probably know when I finally put the dress on and it's just right. Did you know which dress you wanted to wear when you married Dad?"

"I did, but I didn't wear the dress that I wanted. His mother talked me out of it," I said.

"You didn't get to wear the dress you wanted at your own wedding?" Blossom asked, sounding appalled.

I slid into a parking space and turned off the engine. "I didn't, but that was a long time ago." I didn't want to dwell on the topic, mainly because I didn't want to relive my disappointment. I also didn't want to sound as if I was badmouthing her grandmother, though I secretly despised the woman and her domineering personality.

Back then, I had been young and worried about what other people thought. I had wanted a nontraditional dress, but my ex-husband's mother pressured me into wearing traditional white. I didn't listen to my mother, who told me I should do what I wanted since it was my day. I didn't listen to my inner voice, either. The only person's opinion that mattered was Estelle Nabors—because I knew she didn't think I was right for her son, and I desperately wanted her to like me.

The dress did look great on me, and we purchased it at a huge discount, but I wished I had stood my ground and worn the dress I ached to walk down the aisle in.

It had been an explosion of color—mostly maroon and pink shapes against a tan background. Fluid and flowy with long puffy sleeves, it also had a cutaway center that showed off my legs with each step, and when I stood still, the dress pooled at my feet. To this day I regretted my decision.

Conformity had been my priority during that period of my life. At my current age, if I ever walked down the aisle again, I was going to wear what I wanted. I might even try to find my dream dress. That's the kind of conviction that comes with age and no longer being concerned with what other people thought.

As we strolled toward the front of the boutique, I heard, "Auntie Lulah! Blossom!"

Keke raced toward us in jeans and a bright orange shirt, her natural hair worn in a seventies-style Afro. A few years older than Blossom, she was my brother's eldest child and had driven from Indiana, where she now lived, to support Blossom.

After we exchanged hugs—both girls screaming excitedly as if they didn't talk on the phone all the time—we entered the boutique and were greeted by one of the bridal consultants. He wore glasses and a suit and gave his name as Jones. It wasn't clear if that was his first or last name, but we called him Jones since that's how he introduced himself. Not long after, Keke and I were seated on one side of a dressing room that could accommodate two other families.

We waited in our area for Blossom to exit the dressing room in her first dress. "Pretty," Keke murmured, inclining her head toward the other end of the room, where a group of four women and a little girl were oohing and aahing over their family member's pick—a column dress with a sweetheart neckline.

"I'm not crazy about the sleeves, but the rest of the dress is beautiful," I commented.

"Agreed." Keke wiggled her butt on the seat. "These chairs are so comfortable," she remarked.

"I wouldn't mind stealing one on the way out," I said out of the side of my mouth.

"It should fit easily in the back of Orange Julius," Keke said, giggling.

She sipped the non-alcoholic sparkling cider Jones had provided for us. There was also a small tray of grapes, strawberries, and cubed cheeses.

She leaned toward me. "So what do you think about Manuel?"

"I haven't seen much of him, but so far he seems like a nice young man." I kept my answer polite because I knew how close Keke and my daughter were.

"Such a PC answer, Auntie."

I smiled. "I don't know a whole lot about him, so I'm reserving judgment."

"Is he going to get my girl a ring?"

"Blossom said they're going ring shopping later today, so yes."

She sighed. "He should have surprised her. He better not be acting cheap with my cousin."

"How much did she tell you about him and his family?" The girls talked regularly, which was why Keke was here in the first place. Though Blossom had half-siblings, they were much younger and lived in Georgia. She and Keke had a closer, more sisterly relationship.

"Not much. I was surprised when she called and told me she was engaged. Daddy said you were surprised too." She cocked an eyebrow.

"Understatement of the year," I said.

We both laughed.

"As long as she's happy..." Keke said.

I nodded, unable to argue with such a profound statement. "What about you? Seeing anyone?"

"Nothing serious. I have a couple of guys on my roster."

"Excuse me. Does Asher know about this?" I asked, referring to my brother.

"Heck, no. You know how Daddy is. He's chill about everything except when it comes to his kids. Then he turns into a conservative, protective caveman." She rolled her eyes.

My brother could be a bit much at times, but as a parent, I also understood his point of view.

Before I could comment, Blossom came out in her first dress. I knew she had other dresses to try on, but this one already took my breath away.

Keke gasped.

With Jones holding her arm, Blossom carefully stepped up on the bridal pedestal to show off the floor-length mermaid design. The off-the-shoulder neckline skimmed her collarbone and was effortlessly flattering.

"What do you think?" She appeared to be holding her breath.

Keke glanced at me and then back at her cousin. "I love it," she said.

I nodded, struggling to speak because of the lump in my throat. This was happening. My little girl was a grown woman and getting married.

"You look beautiful," I finally managed.

Her face broke into an appreciative smile.

Jones made a few remarks about the fit and places where they could tailor the dress, but overall, we all agreed Blossom looked amazing.

The second dress she tried on was lovely but didn't match the breathtaking beauty of the first one. Neither did any of the others she tried on. By the fifth dress, the three of us knew she was wasting her time. The first gown was "the dress."

While Jones checked to see if they had Blossom's size in stock, she put it on one more time to confirm this was truly what she wanted for her wedding day. Standing on the pedestal, looking at herself in the mirror, her face broke into another smile. "This is the one."

Jones reappeared, and we all looked at him expectantly. He shook his head regretfully.

"If you have to order her dress, will she have it in time for the wedding?" Keke asked.

Jones clasped his hands in front of him and spoke directly to Blossom. "You're not giving me much time to work with, you know that, don't you?"

"Yes, I know," she whispered, her brow wrinkling with worry.

I had the impression Jones was enjoying the tension of this moment.

"We don't have your exact size in stock, and ordering the dress from the designer and then making alterations will take months. You'll be married by the time your gown is ready. But I have an idea," he said, shoving his glasses higher on his nose. "This is our sample gown. If you're willing to buy it, we can start alterations next week."

I held my breath as the room went still, the mirrors reflecting our faces as we all turned our eyes on Blossom.

"I'll take it!" she exclaimed.

Jones's mouth curved upward slightly. "Then I better get to work," he said.

I couldn't take my eyes off my daughter. So sure. So fearless. So excited. For a brief moment, my chest tightened as I envisioned everything that could go wrong.

Then I brushed aside my fears, reminding myself that I had done all I could to raise her well and couldn't protect her forever. At some point, she had to fly on her own.

I wrapped my arms around her and Keke, joining in as they joyously squealed and hugged each other.

Chapter 9

Jamison

"See you later, Jim."

I lifted my hand in a silent goodbye as I exited the state-of-the-art fitness center. I had fallen in love with this facility, a brand-new, sprawling, two-story building that included amenities more impressive than the gym near my condo: group fitness classes, a lounge, a smoothie bar, a salt-water lap pool, and even tanning beds. I said goodbye to my old hangout and never looked back.

Sweat cooling on my skin, I slung my duffel bag over my shoulder and walked into the morning sunshine. I had purposely parked at the opposite end of the lot near the wedding boutique so I could get in extra steps. When I arrived an hour ago, seeing the store had reminded me of Manuel and his pending marriage.

He and Blossom were going ring shopping this afternoon. I still hadn't wrapped my head around the fact that my son was getting married. This was a kid who used to scream bloody murder if I didn't let him wear his Spiderman costume to the grocery store and could never keep up with his shoes, somehow losing one almost every time we left the house. *He* was getting married and about to take on the responsibility of a wife in less than three months and might become a father soon after.

One day, I asked him why the big rush.

"I don't want to wait for the rest of my life to begin," he had said.

His answer surprised and impressed me and made me realize he was more mature than I had given him credit for. He also truly loved Blossom.

As I crossed the lot, three women exiting the boutique caught my attention, and I immediately recognized two of them.

Tallulah and Blossom.

Manuel had told me he and Blossom had worked on the budget and her family had taken on some of the expense. Though relieved, I felt guilty and a bit ashamed of my initial reaction to my son covering the entire wedding expense.

My eyes focused on Tallulah. Her wide-leg pants in a soft, blue shade moved when she walked. The fabric skimmed her hips and legs, relaxed but still showing off her figure. A comfortable yet elegant outfit. The sleeveless white top hugged her torso, and the small crossbody bag nestled between her breasts made me briefly forget how my lungs worked and caused a tightening in my chest.

Flat leather sandals showed off her feet, simple and elegant like her clothes. No heels. I wasn't surprised. She hadn't worn any the other times we met. If I had to guess, she probably preferred to go barefoot.

Her locs were pulled into a loose, sculpted style at the crown of her head, part bun, part art installation, with a few ropey strands framing her face and brushing her neck. Gold hoops caught the light when she laughed, and her wrists were stacked with wood, stone, and metal bracelets. A pendant hung around her neck from black rope, its burnished gold color matching the earrings in her ears.

She glanced in my direction, and her eyes widened in surprise. I couldn't blame her. She probably wondered what the hell she was looking at. Her appearance was flawless. Put together. I, on the other hand, looked like someone who had barely survived leg day.

My tank top was plastered to my chest, and my hair lay flat and lifeless against my head. My gym-issue shorts were unremarkable, reminding me the duffel bag over my shoulder contained a fresh change of clothes I now desperately wished I had utilized.

Oh, and I stunk. As I neared them, I straightened my posture as if that would help. As if standing taller could magically dry my skin, wipe the stank off me, and turn my tank top into a respectable piece of clothing like one of my suits.

"Ms. Washington. Blossom."

"*Hi*," Blossom said, dragging out the word with an odd pitch to her voice.

I couldn't shake the feeling that I intimidated her.

"Hello, Jamison. You were working out, I see," Tallulah remarked.

She assessed me from head to toe. Self-consciously, I combed my damp hair back from my forehead with my fingers.

"Yes. I come here regularly. It's a little out of the way, but it's a great facility." My gaze shifted to the young woman with them who sported an impressive-looking Afro.

"This is my niece, Keke. This is Jamison Harris, Manuel's father."

"Nice to meet you." She extended a hand, and we shook briefly.

"You were dress shopping, I guess? Find anything you like?"

They all three glanced at each other, a smile of satisfaction on each of their faces.

"I did. I chose the first one I tried on," Blossom said.

My eyebrows lifted higher. "I always figured finding the perfect dress took weeks or months of shopping."

"The process does take time, but sometimes women get lucky and find the perfect gown right away. Today happened to be my day," Blossom said. "We're on our way to lunch, and then I'm meeting Manuel to pick out our rings. Next week we have to decide on the venue and the cake. So much to do in a short amount of time."

She didn't seem worried. Excitement glittered in her lovely eyes.

"I'm sure you'll both accomplish what you need to." I stifled a yawn by covering my mouth. I still wasn't sleeping well.

Blossom tilted her head sideways. "Are you okay?" she asked carefully.

"Nothing a short nap won't fix." Assuming I could fall asleep.

"Manuel told me that you suffer from insomnia?"

Great, my son was telling all my business during pillow talk.

"I'm sure it's an easy fix," I said, downplaying the problem. "I made an appointment with a specialist to find out what's going on." Hopefully, they'd give me a prescription to help.

"Maybe you don't need a doctor." Blossom turned toward her mother, an unspoken question in her eyes.

Tallulah shifted from one foot to the other, decidedly uneasy. "I'm sure Jamison is not interested in hearing about any of my ideas."

"You have a solution for insomnia?" I asked, interested despite myself.

"My mother has helped *a lot* of people with her herbal and nontraditional remedies," Blossom said.

"I wouldn't say a lot," Tallulah hedged.

"Thousands. Tens of thousands, I'm sure," her daughter insisted.

Tallulah shot her a *Be quiet* glare, but Blossom wasn't paying attention. I didn't have much confidence in non-traditional solutions. Yes, I took vitamins and believed eating good food was important for good health, but I also believed there were a lot of quacks running around taking people's money and pretending their holistic potions were better than traditional medicine.

"Mom, you probably have something that could help him, right?"

"Jamison said he's going to see a specialist. I'm sure he—"

"I'm interested, actually."

I couldn't believe those words had left my mouth. Neither could Tallulah, apparently, if her raised eyebrows were any indication. Maybe I was more desperate than I wanted to admit. My primary care physician had referred me to a sleep specialist, but my appointment was six weeks away. I had no intention of canceling my appointment, but it couldn't hurt to try something in the meantime. As long as whatever she had in mind wasn't too out of the ordinary, like drinking soup made of bat's wings or sheep's balls.

"I'm not a doctor, but I might be able to help. How long have you been suffering from lack of sleep?" Tallulah asked with what seemed like genuine concern.

"Almost six months," I answered.

"A long time."

Next thing I knew, I was having a consultation in the parking lot. Tallulah asked me a series of questions, and I answered as if I were sitting in a doctor's office. Actually, I don't think a doctor has ever shown as much interest in digging into the source of my problem the way she was. Usually, they made me feel like a number instead of a person, shuttling me in and out as quickly as possible.

I don't know if I really believed Tallulah could help, but I appreciated her interest, and her questions forced me to analyze my situation in a way I hadn't before.

"I have a couple of suggestions," she said at the end of the consultation. "First, don't use your electronic devices right before you plan to go to sleep. Phone, iPad, none of them."

My disappointment in her recommendation must have shown on my face because she pursed her lips.

"Do you want to get better sleep?" she asked.

"I do," I said.

"Try what I'm saying for a couple of weeks and see if there's an improvement. As I was saying, don't use your electronic devices right before going to sleep. The blue light they emit reduces the body's natural production of melatonin, which helps us feel sleepy."

"How long before bed should I stop using my electronics?" I asked, bracing for the worst.

"Start with an hour."

"An hour!" I exclaimed.

"Mom never let me use my phone in bed as a kid, and I do the same now and sleep like a baby every night," Blossom said.

I scratched my head. "Okay, what else?"

"Do you have a programmable thermostat?" Tallulah asked.

"I do."

"Schedule the temperature in your house no higher than sixty-seven degrees at bedtime. Our internal body temperature decreases when we're ready for sleep, and a cool room helps the process and activates sleep-promoting hormones."

She gave a few more suggestions, including doing eye exercises while my eyes were closed, which she demonstrated. I don't know how I didn't laugh. Probably because I was afraid she might punch me if I did.

Finally, she ended with, "The eye exercises don't work for everyone. If they don't, I recommend you take magnesium glycinate, but of course, consult your doctor first. Magnesium glycinate is a calming mineral. It relaxes the brain and is gentle on the stomach."

She had given me quite a list, none of which involved taking drugs. I was intrigued. "Do you recommend any particular brand?"

She gave the names of two brands—one of which I was fairly certain I had seen at my local supermarket—and recommended a dosage.

"Thank you. I'll try your suggestions." I was willing to try anything to get some rest. Sleep deprivation wasn't only causing me to be tired. I also suffered from occasional headaches and figured they'd only get worse.

"If you have follow-up questions, Mom would be happy to help. I mean, we're all going to be family soon." Blossom looked at her mother. "You should give him your number."

Tallulah's smile was tight. "Should I?"

Keke turned away and coughed, which sounded suspiciously like laughing.

"You don't have to give me your number. You've done enough," I said.

"No, Blossom's right. If you have questions, call me, and I'll be happy to answer them." Tallulah removed a sage green card from the small crossbody bag and scribbled a number on the back. "My cell."

To my surprise, she had horrible handwriting. It was like chicken scratch.

I pointed. "Is that a four, or..."

"Six," she said.

"Oh, okay. And, um, this number right here is—"

She interrupted my question, rattling off the entire number. Hopefully, I'd never need to call her because I wouldn't remember what she said.

"Got it. Thank you. I'll leave you ladies alone so you can head to lunch."

We parted ways.

On the way to my car, a silver and orange VW bus passed me, and I wasn't surprised to see Tallulah behind the wheel. An orange and blue dreamcatcher with blue feathers hung from the rearview mirror.

Blossom waved, and I waved back, a smile tugging at the corners of my lips.

Chapter 10

Tallulah

The coffee shop smelled yummy, the perfect combination of espresso and cinnamon. Most people were seated, but a few stood with covered cups of coffee clutched in their hands.

"Hi," I whispered, winding my way between the tables and waving at familiar faces. There were a few dozen people present tonight for the first after-hours tenants' meeting of the small businesses occupying the first and second floors of the recently renamed Freedom Capital Building.

"Hey, Tallulah," Shelley said.

She sat at one of the tables. She and her wife owned Sugar Crumb Bakery on the first floor, and she still wore her gray apron, dusted with flour as if she had stopped in the middle of preparing one of her confectionary masterpieces to come to the meeting. She baked with organic flour and sourced local ingredients as much as she could, like the honey they used in some of the desserts.

"Hi, Shelley, how's it going?"

"Great." Her appearance didn't match her answer.

She looked tired and definitely worried, like the rest of us. Her skin was pale, and though her graying hair was in a ponytail, it looked stringy and greasy as if she hadn't washed it in weeks. "I heard Blossom got engaged. Congratulations."

"Thank you. She's getting married pretty quickly, in less than three months."

"Oh my," Shelley said.

"I know. It's been a whirlwind, believe me, but we found her dress last weekend. One task is completed." I made a check mark in the air.

"Good. Planning a wedding is stressful, especially with a short turnaround."

"Tell me about it," I laughed, edging my way toward the front where Mrs. Chen sat with her purse on her lap.

As I sat down beside her, she leaned over. "I am worried."

I patted her hand. "I'm sure we'll be fine."

Tyler Morris, who owned a UPS-style store offering print, copy, and shipping services, had called the meeting by distributing flyers to all of us. Tyler always had the scoop on everything and everyone. We knew the building was going on the market before the owner notified us because Tyler had already told us. He also informed us when it had sold, days before we received correspondence from the new owner.

Leslie, who ran the coffee shop, stood near the front, hands crossed behind her back, her brown face framed by a cute reddish-blonde pixie. She changed her appearance often with wigs, and every single time they were flattering. She had been in business less than a year and, as far as I could tell, was having success. Whenever I came up to the second floor, she had a steady flow of customers from the professionals upstairs—accountants, consultants, and service providers with predictable incomes who didn't rely on walk-in traffic the way we did on the two lower levels.

Tyler walked to the front and cleared his throat, a few papers in his hands. The hum of conversation in the room died, and everyone paid attention to him.

In his late fifties, his thinning hair was carefully combed over a widening bald spot. He wore wire-rim glasses that constantly slid down his nose, and his shirt was tucked in too tightly, as if he wanted to impress us with a display of authority, though his shoulders curved forward from years of hunching over printing presses.

"I appreciate everyone coming after hours," Tyler said, twisting the stack of papers into a tube.

Not a good sign. He seemed agitated.

"As you know, Freedom Capital Real Estate finalized the buyout last month and renamed the building right away." He rolled his eyes, and soft laughter rippled through the room. "Since the buyout, I've noticed contractors walking the building. Inspectors. People measuring and asking questions."

Zia, who owned a vintage consignment shop, spoke up. "Someone came into my store to inspect the restroom. They might finally fix the toilet I've been complaining about for months."

"Could be good and bad," Tyler said ominously.

My stomach tightened with dread.

"I did some digging," he continued. "Freedom Capital Real Estate has bought up properties in Michigan, Indiana, and Ohio. Same pattern every time. They buy in up-and-coming areas and renovate enough to justify rent increases. As low as twenty-five percent. As high as fifty percent."

The room erupted into gasps and panicked conversations.

"Fifty?"

"Impossible."

"They can't do that!" someone yelled from the back.

Mrs. Chen glanced at me, her hands tightening on her

purse. I had no reassuring words to offer. What he had said was definitely bad news.

"I can't afford such a sharp increase," Shelley said. I glanced over my shoulder and saw her push to her feet. "A twenty-five percent increase would cripple my business. Fifty percent would tank it. We'd have to close up shop. Sales have declined for us every year for the past five years, and we don't know what to do. We tried branching out into edibles to help cover costs, but folks around here aren't interested." She shrugged helplessly and sat down.

A few sympathetic nods followed.

I felt bad for Shelley. Her cakes and breads were delicious. I had no idea she had been struggling with revenue to such a degree. I resolved to talk to Blossom. She hadn't picked a bakery for her wedding cake yet. I'd suggest Shelley's shop.

A male voice piped up from the back.

"Rent increases kind of come with growth, though, right?"

Every head turned.

The owner of the juice shop stood at the back against the glass. Young, athletic, and wearing a vintage T-shirt that probably cost more than my monthly electric bill. His business partner hovered beside him, also young, arms crossed but smiling as if the meeting was a brainstorming session instead of a crisis.

"High rent is sort of the price of being in a revitalizing area, but it'll be good for all of us in the long run."

The room exploded into anger.

"Easy to say. You're funded!"

"Some of us don't have investors!"

"We've been here longer than you've been alive!"

The voices overlapped, accusations flying right and left. One person jabbed a finger into the young man's face. Everyone's reaction was nothing but raw panic masquerading as anger.

I shot to my feet. "Enough." The diatribe continued, and I became deeply concerned the room would soon come to blows. "Enough!" I repeated in a louder voice.

The word cut through the noise, silence followed, and my heart raced a little. I wasn't someone who typically enjoyed being the center of attention, but these were desperate times.

I moved to stand beside Tyler and scanned the room. "We're not enemies. We're neighbors, and yelling at each other won't stop what's coming."

"He doesn't know what he's talking about," someone yelled from the middle of the room.

"There's some truth to what he said, but he doesn't know our specific situation. A huge increase in rent is bad anywhere, but it's especially bad for most of us in this room." I switched my attention to Tyler. "We need more information. A timeline for when we can expect the renovations and the increases. Maybe we could talk Freedom Capital out of the rent increase."

"I don't think so. This is their MO," Tyler said in a grim tone.

"We can try." I returned my attention to the group. "We need to figure out which businesses are most vulnerable to immediate failure and which ones can last a little longer. We decide together, as a group, what we're willing to accept and what we're not."

Slowly, Mrs. Chen nodded, and others did too.

"What we're not going to do is turn on each other. We need to plan."

"I could pull together the research you suggested. Find out how soon after purchase the renovations usually start and how soon after the rent increases take place," Tyler said.

"I'll help you," Zia offered.

Leslie spoke up next. "We should compile a log of when everyone's lease expires and how many years each of us has been in business at this location. I'm one of the newbies, but I don't mind putting together the log if everyone can turn in the information."

More volunteers spoke up, and soon we were hammering out a strategy on how to deal with the landlord and counteract any negative changes coming down the line.

Before the meeting ended, I raised my hand to quiet the group. "One last thing before we leave here tonight. We need to be on the same page and keep our organizing quiet for as long as possible. If the landlord finds out what we're doing before we've had time to put together a strong argument, we run the risk of them coming down hard on us."

Tyler nodded. "No side deals. We're all in this together. United we stand, divided we fall and all that."

Nods of agreement spread through the room.

"You, Tallulah, and Leslie should be our point persons. Captains," Shelley said.

A hum of agreement made its way through the group, along with vigorous head nods.

I glanced at Leslie and Tyler, who both nodded they had accepted their roles.

Feeling more optimistic than when I arrived at the meeting, I said, "We'll be your captains. Communications and suggestions should go through one of us."

I hadn't come here tonight expecting to take on more work, but this was my community. My people. My business, which I had started from practically nothing. First out of my home and then moving to the retail space downstairs. I had poured ten years of blood, sweat, and tears into Simply Well, and I wasn't ready to give up on it yet.

Chapter 11

Tallulah

I placed detox tea, herbal supplements, and two lavender sachets in the bag. "Will that be all for you?" I asked.

"Yes."

Miss Cross was one of my regular customers and had come in for her monthly supply of detox tea and vitamins. She was a real estate agent and always wore tailored suits, with her silver hair styled in a curly bob.

"How is the new landlord? Rumor has it they're planning renovations to the building, which should be good for you and the other tenants. I heard the old landlord was slow to make repairs." She handed over her credit card.

"I'd like to think our situation will improve with the new owners, but we're worried they'll increase the rent and price us out of the building."

Tyler, Leslie, and I had made progress putting together ideas since the tenants' meeting. All the owners had supplied the information we needed for the log, so we knew when all the leases would expire. I had nine months left on mine.

Tyler had learned that renovations typically started small,

with minor improvements like painting and signage changes within sixty days of purchase. During that time, the owners finalized plans for the greater capital expenditures, such as renovating the common areas and upgrading the lighting. By the time they finished with the changes, they could rebrand the building as a luxury location to justify the rent hike.

Miss Cross pursed her lips. "I hope you're wrong, but those tactics are the way of the world nowadays. The big guys force out the little guys. Just know that wherever you land, I'll follow."

"Thanks," I said, shooting her a grateful smile as I tore the receipt off the register.

I hoped I didn't have to leave at all. I wasn't only worried about finding a new place I could afford. I was part of a community here in the building. We all had regular customers and received decent foot traffic because of our location. We supported each other, recommending our products and services to customers, all of which would be lost.

When Miss Cross finished signing, I handed her the bag of products. "Say a little prayer for us."

"I will, and I'm sure you'll be fine. Take care, and I'll see you next month."

As she was the last customer of the day, the door automatically locked behind her.

I hurriedly counted down the register and put the day's deposits in the safe in the back. Blossom had agreed to let Shelley design the wedding cake, and she had roped me into attending the cake tasting with her and Manuel this evening.

So far, the wedding prep was chugging along, though there had been a few hiccups. Since Blossom couldn't contribute financially, she had insisted on planning the wedding instead of hiring a coordinator. A terrible idea, in my opinion, but according to her, she wanted to do more than just show up.

She had chosen Keke as her maid of honor and two friends to be bridesmaids. Somehow, one of her friends from college had assumed she would be in the wedding party, resulting in hurt feelings, a tearful phone call, and Blossom having to reassure her that the only reason she wasn't included was because they had made a decision to have a small wedding.

Then there was the invitation typo fiasco, which I still didn't understand how it had happened. Blossom and Manuel had skipped the formal invitation and sent out digital save-the-date cards directing invitees to the wedding website. Before sending the electronic card, Manuel had reviewed the invitation—so he said. I had also taken a look, and not one of the three of us had caught the typo with the wrong date until Keke called, confused.

We spent two days sending follow-up emails and texts and encouraging everyone to check the website, which always had current information.

Perhaps the most stressful incident had occurred when the green chairs Blossom chose ended up costing significantly more than the plain white ones she had originally seen. She was leaning into an autumn palette for the wedding, which included burgundy, olive green, and terracotta. The combination of colors leaned warm and earthy, making me think of comfort and permanence instead of flash and fuss.

Apparently, more color meant greater cost, and she hadn't wanted Manuel to cover it, so her father and I agreed to take on the additional cost after Karl negotiated them down to a lower price point. Being cheap had its advantages.

I picked up my jacquard-designed cotton bag and slung it over my shoulder. When I was almost to the door, Blossom called.

Wedging the phone between my shoulder and ear, I answered. "Hi, my love."

"Mom, thank goodness I caught you!" she said, sounding out of breath.

I stopped at the door. "What's going on?"

"I'm so sorry, but my interview ran over, and I missed the bus. I'm going to catch a Lyft to the bakery, but unfortunately, I'll be late. Manuel sent me a text, and he's caught in traffic on the other side of town after leaving a client's office. The two of you will have to start the tasting without us."

I immediately tensed, the hairs on the back of my neck standing up. "The two of us?"

"Oh, I didn't tell you? Manuel invited his father since Shelley allows four people at the tasting. Can you handle the appointment until we get there?"

Her announcement had shaken me.

"Of course, but you're only allotted an hour at the bakery. What if you don't arrive on time?"

"Then you and Mr. Harris will have to pick our wedding cake."

"Blossom, I don't know if—"

"Mom, don't sweat it. It's cake. Whatever you choose will be delicious."

"You're sure?"

"Positive. Oh, gotta run! My ride's here. Hopefully, I'll see you soon."

She hung up without saying goodbye, and I remained uncertainly in place, my feet bolted to the floor in apprehension. What was I afraid of? Definitely not the cake. I was honored my daughter trusted me with such an important decision, but that wasn't the reason for my sense of foreboding and the knot in my stomach.

It was because of *him*. Definitely because of Jamison Harris.

He irked me, but I found myself drawn to him. The maturity in his square-jawed face, the soothing sound of his deep voice, his crisp, polished appearance in a suit.

Had I not learned my lesson with my ex? Opposites attract, but they also wear each other down, demanding more compromise than relationships where both parties were alike.

Startled by my thoughts, I stiffened. My attraction, or whatever I felt, was irrelevant. Jamison and I were not in a relationship and were never going to be.

I took a deep breath and fingered the rose quartz around my neck before pushing through the door. Passing by the Far East Market, I waved at Mrs. Chen and her husband behind the register at the front. They wouldn't close up shop until eight.

When I opened the door to Sugar Crumb Bakery, I immediately encountered the enticing aroma of butter and sugar, which temporarily lifted my spirits. Then I saw Jamison. Surprisingly, he was already there, leaning against the display case as he chatted with one of the employees behind the counter.

He wore charcoal slacks and a white shirt with the sleeves rolled up his forearms. No tie or jacket. Casual and relaxed.

I had taken full advantage of observing his body in the parking lot outside the wedding boutique and had been impressed by his physique. He had been sweaty and looking very manly. The vision of his muscular arms and thighs sprinkled with dark hair remained stamped in my brain for hours afterward. Watching him push his sweat-damp hair from his forehead had created a tightening sensation in my chest—and my nipples, if I was being completely honest. Time had seemed to slow with his movements and demand we pay attention.

With each encounter, he stayed top of my mind and appeared more attractive than when we first met. The universe was having a good laugh at my expense because no way was I this attracted to the father of my daughter's fiancé, a man who had made me show my ass in a fine dining establishment.

Jamison straightened when he saw me. "Hello, Ms. Washington."

"Jamison. Have you been here long?" I asked.

"Not too long, but I did leave work early to get here. On the way over, Manuel called and told me he was running late."

"So is Blossom. She had a job interview that took longer than expected."

"Could be a good sign."

"I hope so," I said.

Shelley emerged from the back with her graying hair pulled away from her face. A young woman accompanied her. "Tallulah, hi! And you must be Jamison, Manuel's father?"

"Correct," Jamison said.

"Congratulations to you both on the upcoming wedding. How exciting!"

"Thank you," we said at the same time.

We exchanged a glance.

"Where are Blossom and Manuel?"

"Running a little late but told us to get started," I answered. "If they don't arrive before the session is over, we have permission to select the cake."

"Are you sure?" Shelley asked.

"Yes, but they'll probably be here soon enough," I said.

Shelley clasped her hands together. "Okay then, everything is all set for you to try our cakes. Riley here is going to be taking care of you in our tasting room. She started a few weeks ago as an intern and has been a tremendous help, allowing us to concentrate on finding ways to expand the business."

"You're not staying?" I asked.

Shelley shook her head. "We had a last-minute order come

in yesterday, and I have to deliver it. Have you heard of the rock band Def Panda?"

"I'm not familiar," I admitted.

"They have a show tonight, don't they?" Jamison asked.

The hell? How did he know about a group named Def Panda? A rock band, to boot.

"Yes!" Shelley answered excitedly. "A couple of days ago, we sent their people a box of weed-infused dessert samples. Didn't hear from them until yesterday—last minute, of course, but I'm not complaining. I'm doing a green room delivery of cupcakes, brownies, and they *loved* our lemon bars. I'm so excited! This could be our big break to finally get out of the revenue slump we've been in."

I held up my crossed fingers. "I have my fingers crossed for you."

"Thank you! Anyway, Riley knows which box contains your samples, she has your scorecards, and all you have to do is eat cake and decide which one you like best. Riley, you're good?" She placed a hand on the young woman's shoulder.

Riley gave her a thumbs up. "I got this."

"Perfect. I'm out of here. Jenny, lock the doors in thirty minutes, please," Shelley said to the other young woman behind the counter.

"Will do."

She returned her attention to me and Jamison. "I might be back before you're finished, and hopefully, your kids will arrive in time to try some of the samples."

"We hope," I said.

"See you later." With a quick wave, Shelley disappeared through a door leading to the back of the bakery.

Looking a tad nervous now that her boss was gone, Riley smiled at us. "Follow me, please," she said, leading the way to the tasting room.

Chapter 12

Jamison

I had never been to a cake tasting room before. Never even knew such a thing existed. When I got married, Maria, her best friend, and her sister took care of all the decision-making concerning the food for our wedding. She asked my opinion about a few items, more as a courtesy from what I could tell, but ultimately, the decisions had belonged to her and her closest confidantes.

Sugar Crumb Bakery's tasting room was set off from the main part of the shop, in a small space with two rectangular tables and comfortable-looking chairs. The entire room was painted white, creating the perfect neutral palette to display the colorful dummy cakes and flavor cards on the shelves along one wall.

A glass window cut into the wall separating us from the front of the store allowed a partial view of the bakery and gave customers a glimpse into the room. Riley had set us up at the table farthest from the window, which meant no one could see us, providing a bit of privacy as we indulged.

Basically, I was alone with Tallulah Washington, who, by

the way, looked incredible yet again. Her hair was twisted into a tight bun on top of her head, secured by well-hidden pins. The style lifted her posture and exposed her neck.

She was wearing a luxe-bohemian dress only she could carry off. Fluid and light, it brushed against her body without clinging, just enough to tease. The base color was purple, with multicolored floral and abstract patterns in metallic gold, metallic silver, green, pink, and blue. One shoulder was bare, exposing the graceful line of her collarbone and giving her a regal appearance.

I watched as she set her large purse on the edge of the table and settled into one of the four chairs, her chestnut-brown skin glowing like polished wood, as if she were lit from the inside. My gaze traced the slope of her bare shoulder, and heat curled in my stomach, unexpected and fiery.

I sat down across from her and forced my attention to the task at hand. On the table were sheets of paper, pens, the cake samples, plates, forks, and glasses next to a carafe of water.

"Should we establish criteria to judge the cakes?" I asked, completely out of my depth. I suspected my son had invited me only because Blossom had invited her mother, and he didn't want me to feel left out.

"That's what these are for." Tallulah tapped the sheets of paper.

I paid closer attention to them. They were scorecards for the cakes. Riley had brought in ten samples, and we had to rate each from one to five based on specific criteria—flavor, texture, moistness, appearance, and our overall impression. At the bottom of each sheet was a place to put our names. I immediately wrote my name in the blank.

"By the way, your sleeping tips worked," I said.

Tallulah looked up from writing her name too. "That's good news. Which tips did you follow?"

"I struggled to let go of my electronics the first few nights, but eventually, I buckled down and put them away. It took time for me to fall asleep, but I was able to sleep through the night. I didn't like the eye exercises, by the way. Maybe that's why they didn't work."

"They're not for everyone," she admitted.

"I remember you said that. Anyway, after talking to my doctor, I started on magnesium glycinate."

"And...?" she prodded.

"All I can say is, damn, magnesium, where have you been all my life?"

She laughed, which prompted a smile from me. It felt really good to make her laugh. Why did it feel so good?

"Now I fall asleep fast, sleep through the night, and wake up rested. I haven't had a headache in over a week. So, Ms. Washington, I canceled the appointment with the specialist my doctor referred me to. Unless something changes, I don't need to see him. Thank you."

"You're welcome," she said softly.

Tension drained from my body. Our polite, friendly exchange was a turning point. Our initial meeting had been adversarial, but clearly, we could be cordial.

"We only have an hour, so do you want to get started?" Tallulah asked.

"Sure. Which one?"

"How about this?" She pointed to the cake labeled *classic vanilla bean.*

Much more relaxed than when I had arrived, I picked up a fork. "Let's do this."

I put a morsel in my mouth and chewed. Tasted good but simple, was moist, and sweet without being sugary. I made an involuntary, appreciative sound.

A faint smile touched Tallulah's lips. What color was on

her mouth? It was deeper than red and emphasized the plump lusciousness of her lips.

"I agree. Solid choice, in my opinion."

"Not bad at all." I graded the cake and wrote additional feedback in the notes section of the scorecard.

"Do you want to pick the next one?" she asked.

I eyed the options. "How about the lemon with raspberry filling?"

"Never a bad choice."

We tried the sample. I wrinkled my nose.

"You don't like it?" Tallulah asked.

"It's not terrible. A little tart for my taste."

"Interesting. To me, the flavors are perfectly blended."

We graded the cake and wrote our notes. Next was an almond cake with Biscoff buttercream.

We tried the sample.

"Damn," we both said at the same time.

Then we burst into laughter.

"Imagine that, the two of us agreeing on something," I said.

"We didn't have a choice. This is unbelievably good. Moist, great flavor, not too sweet."

"I don't want anything else. This is it. Check, please."

Tallulah laughed at my joke. If she kept laughing, I had no choice but to keep making jokes.

I scraped leftover crumbs and icing from the plate, and she tried to block me. We ended up in a playful silverware battle, fighting for the last bit of our favorite so far.

Next was a chocolate cake with chocolate ganache, which we both agreed was too rich.

We tried the honey lavender cake next. As I chewed, I noticed the flavor was a little off. The cake was decent, with a floral note that didn't overwhelm, but there was another flavor underneath I was struggling to identify.

"Do you taste that?" I asked.

Tallulah nodded, her expression becoming contemplative.

"Kinda earthy, isn't it?" I asked.

"I was going to say herbal."

"Like rosemary, or..." I struggled to find the words for the unfamiliar taste.

"Something else. I don't think it's the lavender, either. Shelley uses a lot of organic ingredients and local honey. Could be something local we're not familiar with," she suggested.

"Hmm. Maybe."

We both sat there for a moment, chewing slowly.

Riley popped her head in the door. "Everything okay in here?"

"We're fine. There was an unusual herbal flavor in the lavender honey cake. Any idea what it could be?" Tallulah asked.

"No, ma'am, but I'll ask Shelley when she comes back."

"No need. I was just curious."

"If you don't have any more questions, I'll help Jenny close up shop."

"Go ahead, you don't need to babysit us. We know where to find you if we need help."

After she left, I raked my gaze over the choices left. "What's next?"

"There's one filled with strawberry. Let's try it," Tallulah said.

We tried another piece of cake and another, and after a while, I began to feel... odd. I wasn't sure exactly what was going on, but I felt myself slowing down and the edges of the room became... softer.

I leaned back in the chair. "I am so relaxed right now." Was I talking slower?

Tallulah laughed. Then I laughed.

The two of us kept laughing.

"Why was that so funny?" I asked.

"I don't know. I guess because I feel really relaxed too." She covered her mouth and giggled uncontrollably.

I tapped her cotton bag sitting on the table. "Pretty. I liked the one you had at Knife & Fork too. How many of these bags do you have?" What the hell was wrong with me, telling her how much I liked her accessories? I was out of control.

"These bags?"

Was she slurring her words? Was I?

"Um..." She tapped her chin and gazed up at the ceiling, taking forever to answer. I might have briefly fallen asleep. "At least thirty."

"Thirty!" I exclaimed, so loudly she jumped. "Thirty is a lot," I said, dropping my voice to a whisper.

"I know. I love them so, so, so much. They're the best. Comfortable, go with anything, and can hold..." Her brow wrinkled.

I tilted my head. "Something wrong?"

She rubbed a hand across her eyes. "I forgot what I was about to say."

"Me too."

"You forgot what I was about to say?"

"Yeah. I think..." What I said didn't make sense.

We stared at each other in confusion for a moment and then burst into uncontrollable laughter.

"I feel so goddamn good right now." I pointed at the ceiling. "Four score and seven years ago..."

Tallulah snorted in laughter. "What are you doing?"

"I think I'm quoting the Gettysburg Address. Am I?"

"I have no idea."

Trying to ground myself, I took a sip of water and then

placed the glass on the table with extra care. "I'm not feeling like myself right now."

"Me neither."

We stared at each other. Then our gazes lowered to the remaining samples. I lifted my eyes, she lifted her eyes, and we locked gazes.

"The cakes," we said simultaneously.

"Oh, shit," Tallulah said, slapping her forehead and laughing. "Rhonda gave us the wrong samples. I mean, Riley."

We burst into laughter again. What a mess. We were supposed to be deciding on a wedding cake. Instead, we were sitting in a bakery, possibly high, laughing like a couple of hyenas.

"No more cake for you," Tallulah said, reaching for her water.

"You either," I said.

I watched her drain the glass, tilting her head way back. A line of water dribbled down her chin. My lips parted, and my tongue thrust forward. I ached to lick the water from her skin.

She wiped it off the way little kids do—with the back of her hand.

We both looked at each other across the table. She truly did have the most beautiful brown eyes, and her lips were temptingly full. My eyes traced the curves of her mouth—the soft bow of her upper lip, the fuller swell of the lower one. I had the sudden, demanding urge to know how they felt beneath mine.

"Jamison." She said my name in a soft voice, as if asking me a question.

"Yes?"

"We should probably let them know we're finished."

My eyes shifted to a light speck on her dark skin. "You have a little bit of frosting..." My voice was thick and heavy.

"Where?"

"Let me show you."

I staggered to my feet and swayed a little but held onto the table for balance. Dropping into the chair beside her, I leaned forward, bringing my face inches from hers.

"Right. Here," I whispered huskily, brushing my thumb against her soft cheek.

She didn't withdraw, and my hand lingered.

Her eyes dropped to my mouth, and my stomach reflexively tensed. I was thinking of doing the unthinkable. I was thinking of kissing this woman.

My gaze swept over the fullness of her lips, and a yawning ache expanded inside me.

"Jamison." She said my name in a trembling whisper. An invitation, no doubt.

Her eyelids lowered and her mouth tilted up toward mine.

"Mom?"

I jerked back so fast, my elbow knocked the carafe off the table and sent water and glass splashing all over the floor.

Chapter 13

Tallulah

"I can't believe this happened. I'm so sorry!" Shelley exclaimed. She had arrived shortly after Manuel and Blossom.

"It's okay. Really." My head was buzzing, and I held onto Blossom to maintain my balance.

"No, it's not, Tallulah," Shelley insisted.

Jenny was in the back cleaning up the spilled water and broken glass. The rest of us stood at the front of the shop—Jamison and Manuel, Blossom and me, and Shelley and Riley, whose eyes were red-rimmed.

Jamison and I had guessed correctly. Riley had given us the wrong samples. Each one was color-coded, and she had put out samples from a green-labeled box, which contained cannabis-infused samples, instead of the gold-labeled box, which contained the wedding cakes. The honey lavender cake had been the only sample where the herbal flavor of the drug had been detectable. Riley had apologized profusely, but the damage was done.

Frankly, I wanted to get out of there as soon as possible. I was one of those few people in the world who had a low tolerance for weed, a problem I discovered in my youth. Since then, I hadn't touched the drug, but based on memories, I knew the high would last for a long time, and afterward, I'd probably have a headache. All I wanted to do was go home and go to bed. Mmm... sleep sounded like such a good plan right now.

"Why are the two of you smiling so much?" Blossom demanded.

I was smiling? I perked up and fixed my face.

"Because they're high off edibles," Manuel said, glancing at his father.

"The cakes were good, by the way. Especially the almond cake. *Yummmm,*" Jamison said.

I looked at him. He looked at me.

Despite everything that had occurred—Blossom's shocked voice, the way Jamison and I guiltily jumped back from each other, and Manuel's confused expression as he stood behind my daughter—I started laughing again.

Jamison hid his face in his hands, his shoulders bouncing up and down as he chuckled.

Manuel rolled his eyes like a disgruntled parent. "We need to get them home."

"Good idea," Blossom said, gripping my arm, as if I were a misbehaving toddler.

"Tallulah, I'll call you," Shelley said.

"Bye," I sang, turning and waving as I was whisked away by my daughter, who seemed very strong all of a sudden.

Jamison and I locked eyes before I was tugged through the door, and time stopped. My heart contracted, and heat spread throughout my chest. The dynamic between us had shifted, and though in a woozy state, I was certain our relationship wouldn't be the same again.

Blossom helped me into Orange Julius, and we drove home

in silence, my head resting against the cool window, eyes closed. Eventually, the drug would pass through my system, and I'd be back to normal. I just needed to rest.

I must have dozed off because one minute we were bumping along the road, and the next, Blossom was shaking me awake.

"We're home," she said, unhooking her seatbelt. "Don't move. I'm coming around to help you."

"I can walk," I muttered, fumbling with the belt. It wouldn't budge. I tugged angrily to get it loose. Great. I insisted I could walk but couldn't get out of the seatbelt.

Blossom opened my door and unsnapped the buckle with ease. She helped me out, and we slowly walked into the house.

"Are you going to be okay?" she asked as she escorted me down the hall.

"Take me to my bed, and I'll be fine."

In my room, she helped me undress, removed my shoes, and tucked me in.

"I'll check on you later."

"All right, my love," I whispered.

I sensed her standing over me but couldn't open my eyes. Being in bed seemed to have a dramatic effect on my ability to lift my lids. I simply couldn't, as if they were glued shut.

I sighed and finally fell asleep.

* * *

At almost midnight, I woke up, and as suspected, I had a headache. Now that I was safely in my own space, I replayed what had occurred.

I may have been high, but there was no denying what had happened between me and Jamison. I had almost kissed him over an almost empty platter of weed cake samples.

When he leaned in, I should have pulled back or made a joke to diffuse the situation, but the warm pressure of his thumb on my skin had hypnotized me, and my entire body had tingled with anticipation. With a clearer mind, I was mortified we had practically been caught in a compromising position.

I sat up and winced as the pounding in my head intensified. Shuffling into the bathroom, I stared bleary-eyed at my reflection, wearing only a bra and cotton underwear.

"You look a mess," I told my reflection.

I splashed cool water on my face to wake up and rinsed my mouth with clove water. Back in my room, I pulled on a pair of baggy shorts and an oversized shirt and padded down the hall to the kitchen. I was dying of thirst and starving.

Blossom was sitting at the table with her laptop and magazines spread out before her.

"Hey, Stoner, how are you feeling?" she asked.

I paused to glower at her and pointed with my forefinger. "Don't make jokes. I was an innocent victim."

I drank two glasses of water and tossed back a couple of magnesium pills to help with the headache. If they didn't eliminate the pain in an hour or so, I'd take something stronger.

"What are you working on?" I opened a can of sardines and mashed them on a plate. Though I was hungry, I didn't want to have to cook anything. Sardines with crackers and a piece of fruit should hold me until the morning.

"Doing a little planning," Blossom answered. "Manuel has a lot of family on both sides, and it seems as if every single one of them wants to come to the wedding."

"Can you accommodate them at the venue?" I asked.

"I think so," she said slowly, eyes glued to the computer screen. "We have a few logistical issues to work out, but the good news is Mr. Harris has agreed to pay for the rehearsal dinner, so that's one less expense we have to worry about."

She looked up as I walked over to the table with my food.

"Sardines, sourdough bread, and a peach. Quite the meal you have there," Blossom said.

"If I didn't know better, I'd say you were enjoying my discomfort."

"Only a little bit. It's kind of funny that some edibles kicked your butt like that."

"I have a low tolerance, which I learned when I was your age. The high is more intense for people like me, and so are the aftereffects."

"Mr. Harris must have a low tolerance too. He was definitely out of it." Blossom flipped the page of one of the magazines.

"Neither he nor I would have been at the bakery getting high if not for the two of you. By the way, I wanted crackers with my sardines. Where are they? There was a whole sleeve in the pantry the other day."

"Oops. I forgot to mention we were out." Blossom watched me with interest. "So, you and Mr. Harris—"

"Whatever you're about to say—"

"Can I finish?"

I tensed, shoving a piece of sardine-covered bread into my mouth.

"You and Mr. Harris looked mighty friendly when Manuel and I walked in. I guess you're getting along a lot better now?"

I avoided her eyes and focused on my food. "He's not as bad as I originally thought, and he has a somewhat good sense of humor." I shrugged.

"He's not bad looking, either."

I lifted my gaze, and Blossom arched an eyebrow. "What are you doing?"

"What were *you* doing?" she countered.

"I was eating cake because my daughter was running late from an interview. Whatever you think you saw—"

"What do you think I think I saw?"

"Time for this conversation to come to an end. Do you need me to help you with the planning?" I gestured at everything on the table.

Quietly smug, she smiled. "No, I'm good for now. Glad you're feeling better."

"I'll feel a lot better in the morning once I've had a full night's sleep." I paused. "Have you heard from Manuel how his father is doing?" Considering her teasing, I hated to ask, but I was curious.

"He texted me and said his dad had gone straight to bed, like you."

"That's probably best." I picked up my plate and went to pour myself another glass of water. Taking my food, I headed toward the door. "I'm going to my room. You're sure you don't need my help?"

"I'm sure. Get some rest, Mom."

"You too. Don't stay up too late working on wedding plans. We can figure out the seating charts and whatever else you have going on tomorrow, okay?"

"Thanks."

I strolled back to my room and kicked the door shut with the heel of my foot. Sitting cross-legged on my comforter, I bit into the peach.

The drugs had had an interesting effect on me once they kicked in. I had become aware of Jamison in pieces. Like the way his shoulders had relaxed out of their usual rigid line. His gray eyes were lighter than I originally noticed and observed me with blatant interest. The way he wrote his notes and graded the cakes. I could tell he took the whole process probably more seriously than necessary.

Then there was the almost-kiss. My body ached with regret. My core throbbed with unresolved sexual tension.

Sighing, I leaned back against the pillows and closed my eyes, the peach forgotten in my hand. I relived the moment Jamison touched me and the way the world narrowed to the small space between us. The next time I saw him, should I pretend nothing happened?

I had carefully dodged the conversation Blossom tried to have about Jamison, but there was no escaping the truth. The drugs had stripped away my defenses, but they didn't invent the feelings I had experienced.

I wanted Jamison Harris. My daughter's future father-in-law.

That was a problem.

Chapter 14

Tallulah

It didn't work.

I frowned as I read the message from Donna, a new customer who had come in a few days ago. The store was closed, and I was responding to emails before I went home. According to Donna, the collagen peptides I had recommended for her joint pain hadn't worked.

I tapped out an answer, explaining they weren't a one-time fix and she had to take them regularly. I encouraged her to continue adding the powder to her smoothies and other beverages, and she should notice a gradual improvement.

When I finished, I jotted a few notes for the winter reset class I taught each year. One night a week for four weeks, I educated first-timers and regulars on how to support their immune system during the winter months, manage stiffness as the weather changed, and improve their energy and mood as the days became shorter.

After closing the store, I waved to Mrs. Chen and her husband as I left. As usual, being alone with my thoughts thrust me back in time to the incident at the bakery. Since then, Shelley had stopped in twice at my center to apologize and offered to bake the wedding cake for free.

The first time, I gave her a firm *No.* The second time she came in, it was clear she wouldn't be satisfied until she had somehow rectified the situation. But we were friends, and while what happened had been a horrible mistake, it was a mistake nonetheless. I didn't want to take advantage of her guilt and offered to pay half price for the cake, which she accepted.

We were both happy. I received a discount on the cake, and she got the peace of mind she had been craving—which I hadn't been able to achieve myself.

My mind inevitably drifted to what happened between me and Jamison last Friday evening. Well, nothing had actually *happened*, but I was definitely more aware of him. My face burned with embarrassment at the thought of us almost locking lips, and we would have if our kids hadn't arrived when they did.

Manuel had told Blossom that his father had suffered the ill effects of the edibles as well. Though he had slept through the night, when Manuel checked on him the following morning, he had been nauseous and only able to eat crackers until his appetite came back around the middle of the day. If I had to guess, he suffered from a low tolerance to cannabis. Something we had in common.

Eventually, I put Jamison out of my mind and spent the rest of the ride home contemplating the upcoming wedding. By the time I parked in the driveway, I had a few ideas to run by Blossom.

Walking through the door, the appealing scent of simmering spaghetti sauce filled with basil and garlic greeted me.

"Mom, is that you?" Blossom called out.

"No, I'm a serial killer," I called back, heading toward the kitchen.

She was standing at the stove, a small spoon near her lips. "Not funny," she said, before tasting the sauce.

I placed my satchel on the table, which was once again strewn with magazines and sheets of paper as she planned her big day.

I sat down. "How is it?" I already knew the sauce was delicious. My daughter was a great cook. She took after me.

"Yummy." She did the happy booty dance she had been doing since she was a teen and then tossed the spoon in the sink. "Dinner is almost ready. I'll let the sauce simmer for a few more minutes."

"Thanks for cooking," I said.

She shrugged. "It's the least I could do since I'm mooching off you."

"You're my daughter. You're not mooching."

"I don't have a job. I'm not paying rent. I'm not paying *any* bills." She counted each item on her fingers. "Mooching."

"One more time, you are my daughter. You are *always* welcome here, whether or not you're working."

Leaning against the counter, she rested her hands on her hips and smiled appreciatively. "Thanks, Mom."

"That includes in the future, if your marital situation changes."

She rolled her eyes. "You couldn't help yourself, could you? When are you going to accept that just because Manuel and I are getting married quickly, it doesn't mean we don't love each other?"

"I'm aware. I'm your mother, probably the most open-minded person you know. But I'm simply pointing out your situation could change in the future. Your father and I were in love too. Your cousin Jay-Jay and his wife were in love. Things change, people change, situations change, and one day you might want to walk away. I want you to know my door is always open for you. This is a soft place for you to land."

"Thanks, but I'm confident it won't be necessary."

I didn't want to belabor the point and dampen her happiness. "I guess not, since Manuel bought you a ginormous ring," I teased.

She and Manuel had finally found a set of rings they both loved.

"It's nice, isn't it?"

Blossom shoved her hand in my face, her finger weighted down by a rock the size of Gibraltar. A gorgeous diamond was set in a platinum band, clear and princess-cut. He had more than made up for not buying her a ring in the first place.

I squinted, pretending to shield my eyes from the glare. "Where are my sunglasses?"

Blossom laughed, happier than I had ever seen her. Slowly, the smile faded from her face. "I need to talk to you about something," she said.

"Uh-oh. Sounds serious."

"It's not a big deal, but you're probably not going to like what I have to say."

"Okay," I said, definitely worried now.

"Manuel and I have a few dances planned for our day. The wedding party has agreed to do a short dance number going into the reception, so they're working with a choreographer for the routine."

I wrinkled my nose.

"Mom, I don't care if you like the idea or not. It's my wedding."

I shrugged. I had no desire to talk her out of her plans since dancing into the reception was common practice nowadays.

"Then, of course, Manuel and I have our first dance, which will be to a salsa tune. He wants to pay homage to his Hispanic side, and we'll work with a private instructor to make sure we get the moves right."

"I'm not hearing the part where I should be worried," I said.

She clasped her hands together and looked me directly in the eyes. "We want you and Mr. Harris to take a class too."

I burst out laughing. "There is no way I'm dancing into the reception, my love. There are a lot of things I would do for you, but *that* is not one of them."

"Believe me, I know you won't and that you hate the whole idea of a choreographed dance at a reception. But this is more about... skills."

I frowned. "I don't understand."

"Manuel is going to dance with his mother and then you. I'm going to dance with Dad and then Mr. Harris. Mr. Harris is not the best dancer, so we wanted him to take a class."

"What does that have to do with me?" I asked, completely confused.

"You can't dance, Mom."

My mouth fell open. "What are you talking about? I'm a great dancer."

She bit her bottom lip. "No, you're not. So we want you to take lessons too."

"Tell me you're kidding."

"It's only four nights, and—"

"I know how to dance!" I exclaimed.

Blossom inhaled deeply and let out her breath slowly, as if trying to contain her temper. "No, you don't. Everyone in the family calls you Rhythmless Nation."

"*Excuse me*? Who calls me Rhythmless Nation?"

"Everybody."

"Who is everybody, Blossom?" I demanded, my voice raised.

"Now you're mad."

"I am not mad!" I yelled. I was mad. "I simply want to know who the hell in the family has been calling me Rhythmless Nation behind my back?"

"Do you really want to know?"

"Isn't that what I said?" I snapped.

"Okay, it's Jay-Jay, Uncle Desmond, Uncle Marcus, Auntie Agnes, Grandpa—"

My hand shot up. "Stop."

How humiliating. Maybe I wasn't the best dancer and didn't know the steps to every single line dance that came out every single year—there were so many of them!—but *Rhythmless Nation*? That was plain cruel.

Blossom sat on my lap.

I ignored her.

She looped her hands together behind my neck. "I love you, Mommy."

"Not gonna work," I said, looking past her.

"*Mom.*"

I sighed and finally met her gaze.

"Don't be upset. Look at this as an opportunity to prove everyone wrong. The lessons start the week after next, and all you have to do is take the four classes with Mr. Harris—two the first week and two the week after. You'll be learning the waltz."

"You've already signed us up?"

Embarrassed, color filled her cheeks. "The lessons were Manuel's idea. He was paying for the classes for his dad, and then I mentioned you might kinda need classes too, so we added your name. Couples receive a discount."

"We're not a couple," I said, warmth flooding my torso at

being referred to as a couple with Jamison. At having to *dance* with him.

"You only have to go for four nights. We don't want you guys to be embarrassed when you have to bust a move at the wedding."

"What you mean is, you don't want us to embarrass you."

"Maybe," she said in a low voice, looking sheepish. "Please, Mom. Do this for me." She batted her lashes and gave me the puppy dog eyes that used to melt me and her father when she was a kid. Unbelievably, the trick still worked.

"Fine," I muttered.

"Yay! Thank you!"

She hugged my neck and pressed her cheek against mine, and I hugged her back. The things we do for our kids.

"Now get up off me. You're heavy." I playfully shoved her, and she hopped off my lap. "I'm going to change out of these clothes."

"By the time you come back, dinner should be ready. I have garlic bread in the oven too. Oh, and I'll show you some of my ideas for the wedding. Manuel and I have been arguing about the menu."

"I have some ideas for you too." I picked up my satchel as I stood. "I thought you had already decided on the menu."

"We did, but I had a different idea that could save money. A food truck!" She made the announcement with excitement, her eyes bright.

"A food truck?"

She nodded vigorously. "It's common practice now."

"So I've heard. What's the problem? You want the truck but Manuel doesn't?"

"No, he wants a pizza truck, but I think tacos will be better."

"Quite the dilemma," I said with a laugh. "Give me a few

minutes. I definitely want to hear more about this, and you need to come to a decision. You don't have a lot of time."

"I know," Blossom wailed.

"I'll be right back."

As I walked to my bedroom, I sighed, lifting my eyes heavenward.

Dance classes. With Jamison.

What could possibly happen next?

Chapter 15

Jamison

Dance lessons. As if I didn't have anything better to do.

I arrived at Elegant Dance Studio fifteen minutes early, giving me enough time to second-guess my decision to come at all. Not that I really had a choice. Manuel had made it clear that coming was not optional.

"Dad, I remember you standing against the wall at every party we went to when I was a kid. You're not doing that at my wedding. You're dancing with Blossom."

In my defense, most of those parties were thrown by the Mexican side of his family, and I was no Latin dancer. I saved myself and Maria embarrassment by holding up the wall and occasionally moving my shoulders as if I were too cool to get out on the floor.

The main reason I was hesitant to be here tonight was because of what had happened between me and Tallulah a couple of weeks ago. How was I supposed to be in close proximity to her and act like a normal, functioning adult when all I could think about were her lips and the softness of her skin when I unnecessarily wiped frosting from her cheek?

After a long delay where I watched couples arrive and go inside, I climbed out of my Lexus and shut the door. The studio occupied the second floor of a converted warehouse that housed a number of businesses geared toward the arts—among them an art gallery, a pottery studio, and the dance studio.

Staring up at the brightly lit windows from the parking lot, I saw two of the students already practicing their steps.

"I should leave," I muttered to myself.

As I plotted a plan of escape by feigning an emergency, Tallulah's orange bus pulled into the parking lot, and she parked two spaces away. When she stepped down from the vehicle, I had to remind myself to breathe normally.

Like every other time I had seen her, she wore a colorful outfit. This time, it was a burnt orange skirt that landed right below her knees, paired with a cream tank top. Her locks were gathered into a high ponytail and wrapped in a colorful fabric that matched her skirt. Silver bracelets on both her wrists chimed against each other with each movement. Turquoise earrings—which were actual chunks of turquoise suspended from silver chains, not the delicate studs I often saw other women wearing—hung from each lobe.

Along with the ring in her nose, her entire appearance was earthy and feminine—like a sexy Mother Earth. I should not be noticing this much.

She observed me from a few feet away. "You came."

"Manuel had a compelling argument for my attendance," I said, slipping a hand into the pocket of my slacks, trying to look casual despite tensing at her appearance.

"Blossom said I have no rhythm and suggested I would embarrass her if I didn't take lessons." She winced.

"You lack rhythm?" I couldn't believe it.

She cocked her head. "Why do you sound so surprised?"

"Because you're..." I caught myself before I said what was on the tip of my tongue.

One of her eyebrows arched higher. "Yes?" she prompted.

"Nothing," I mumbled.

"Is it because I'm *buh-lack*?" she asked, the same eyebrow stretching higher.

"I did not say a word about your ethnicity."

She stared at me for a second and then started laughing. I relaxed and breathed easier.

"I'm not offended. My daughter offended me, if I'm being honest, and apparently my entire family agrees I have no rhythm."

"At least you only have a lack of rhythm to contend with. Apparently, I'm a two-for. No rhythm *and* I don't know how to move my hips." I grimaced.

She covered her mouth as she laughed, and this time I arched my eyebrow.

"I can at least move my hips," she explained.

My gaze swept her body. The tank top clung to her breasts and torso, revealing womanly curves. My eyes traveled lower, to where the skirt draped over her hips.

Wouldn't mind seeing those hips move, I thought.

When I lifted my eyes, she was looking right at me. Instead of glancing away, I held her gaze. I was embarrassed but decided I wouldn't feel guilty for noticing she was an attractive woman with a great figure. I wasn't blind.

She looked away first. "Seems we're both here under duress."

"A unifying factor," I remarked.

Neither of us moved toward the entrance, and though several feet separated us, I felt her presence as if she were standing right next to me. The last time we had been alone, my thumb had been at the corner of her mouth, and I had been seconds away from—

"We should go in," Tallulah said.

"We should."

Instead of taking the elevator, we walked up the stairs. The studio was much larger than I had appreciated when standing in the parking lot looking up through the windows. The walls were made of exposed brick and the floors of hardwood. Mirrors lined one wall, and a sound system was set up in one of the corners.

I didn't see anyone who appeared to be the teacher, but four couples were already ahead of us. They nodded and smiled as we entered. Two of the women greeted us with a soft "Hello."

One of the couples appeared to be younger than Tallulah and me by at least ten years. They wore matching athletic gear. Another couple seemed about our age, but the other two couples were in their sixties, and one of them practiced their moves, gliding across the floor with the fluid ease of people who have probably been dancing together for decades. It made me wonder why they were in this class, which was supposed to be for beginners.

A few minutes later, a woman entered the room, and I knew right away she was the instructor. She appeared to be in her early sixties, with a buzz cut of white hair and wearing a leopard-print leotard to show off her tight, lithe body.

She glided across the floor. "Good evening," she said.

"Good evening," we all chorused.

"Welcome, and thank you all for coming. I am Carmen Lundgren, and I will be your instructor this evening. Before we start, I'll tell you a little bit about myself, and then I'd like for each of you to introduce yourselves and tell me why you're taking this class."

She gave us a brief history of her career in dance, which she started as a hobby, eventually becoming a professional and dancing in the United States and around the world. When she retired, she opened this studio with her husband, also a dancer.

She pointed to each of us in turn, and we explained why we were taking the class. Tallulah and I were the only ones preparing for a wedding. I learned that the older couple I had seen practicing earlier was taking the class because they danced for exercise, but the wife had suffered an injury a month ago and they were taking it easy until she was back to normal.

"Now I understand why you're all here. Tonight you're going to learn the basics of the waltz. It's elegant and perfect for wedding receptions." She glanced in our direction and then clapped her hands. "We're going to start with the frame position."

She showed us the move and then instructed us to get into position.

Tallulah and I faced each other. I'm not sure my heart had ever beaten this fast in my life.

Rolling my shoulders, I forced myself to relax. This was fine. I could handle a little dance. We were two adults learning a skill for the benefit of our children. So what if I couldn't stop looking at her plump, red lips?

"Right hand on the shoulder blade," Carmen said, demonstrating with the younger couple. "Left hand extended, then you hold your partner's right hand. Ladies, please place your left hand on your partner's shoulder, and do keep some space between you. This is not a slow grind at the prom."

There was a little bit of laughter as we all moved into position.

I carefully placed my right hand onto Tallulah's back, on her shoulder blade. Her skin was warm through the fabric of her tank top. She lifted her hand onto my shoulder, and her touch branded me, searing through my dress shirt. Our other hands met in the air between us.

"Well done!" Carmen strolled between the couples, making sure everyone was in the right position. "Now ladies, I must tell you that in this dance, equality goes out the window. You must follow where the man leads. Gentlemen, she is following your lead, so you must know what you're doing, okay? The waltz is a box step, which means you form a box pattern on the floor with your feet. Watch me, please. One, two, three. Again, one, two, three. First we'll try this without music, and then I will add the music. On my three count: one, two, three, begin."

Tallulah stepped back, and I stepped forward. My foot landed directly on her toes, and she grimaced.

"Damnit!" I said. "Sorry."

"It's fine," she said.

"One, two, three," Carmen was saying.

We waited until she restarted the count and jumped in. This time, I stepped to the side too quickly, and Tallulah stumbled trying to follow.

I gripped her hand, pulling her close to keep her from falling. Her soft breasts pressed against my chest, and I inhaled sharply before she quickly stepped back.

My dick jumped. *Please don't let me get a hard-on in this class*, I prayed.

"Don't think so hard," Tallulah said.

"I'm trying not to maim you." I smiled through the clenching of my teeth. *And trying not to get a hard-on in this class*, I mentally added.

"You're going to grind down your molars doing that all the time," she remarked.

Startled, I stared. "Doing what?"

"The fake smile thing you do when you grit your teeth."

"You noticed?" It was a bad habit.

"A blind woman could see what you're doing," she said. My wife never did. "You don't miss much, do you?"

"I try not to."

We started moving again with stiff, awkward steps.

Carmen appeared beside us. "You two, stop."

We froze.

Uh-oh.

Chapter 16

Jamison

"Why are you so tense?" Carmen asked. Then, without waiting for an answer, she adjusted my elbow and Tallulah's posture. "This is not a business meeting. This is dance. You must feel the movement."

"I don't really do feeling things," I groused.

She stepped back, eyeing us critically. "You will have to learn... Jamison, is it?"

"Yes," I answered, feeling properly chastised.

She studied us, then lifted her hands, measuring the distance between our bodies. "I need you closer together."

"But you said we shouldn't be too close," Tallulah reminded her.

Did I hear panic in her voice?

"I did, but there is no need to act as if you're maintaining social distance protocols. I need you a little closer together, please."

Tallulah shuffled closer, and so did I. Now there were only inches between us, and my nostrils captured the distinctive fragrance she wore. It was sweet, not cloying like the overwhelming perfumes some women tended to wear. A warm, sweet, inviting fragrance. Dangerously so.

A smile swept across Carmen's lips. "Much better. Now, Jamison, I need you to close your eyes, please."

I swung my head in her direction. "What did you say?"

"Close. Your. Eyes. Trust me."

Obviously, I didn't trust her, but I reluctantly did as she asked, feeling absolutely ridiculous.

"You too, Tallulah."

I tried to relax, but I couldn't. I was acutely aware of every point of contact between me and Tallulah. My hand on her back, her hand on my shoulder, our palms pressed together in the air.

"Good," Carmen said, her voice sounding closer and softer. "I want you to sway back and forth. *Gently*. Don't move from your position. Just sway. Jamison, you start and guide your partner."

Once again, I did as she asked.

"Good, good. Just like that. Continue to move, don't think about it too much. Feel the motion and let your body guide you. Now, add the steps. Remember, Jamison is leading. One, two, three. Yes, yes. One, two, three."

Behind the darkness of my eyelids, I was not allowed to overthink the mechanics of the steps, and it made a difference. Tallulah followed me naturally, responding to the smallest pressure of my hand on her back. When I stepped forward, she stepped back. When I shifted right, she glided right along with me.

"Now, open your eyes," Carmen continued in the same soft voice.

I opened my eyes, and Tallulah was looking at me, her expression unguarded. Similar to how she had looked in the bakery when we were both high. Her lips were slightly parted, and her turquoise earrings swayed with our movements.

"There you go," Carmen said, backing away. "Continue to dance like that. One, two, three."

We shuffled across the floor, maintaining the connection we had found when our eyes were closed and we were entrenched in darkness.

"You're not doing too badly," my partner remarked.

"You're doing a good job yourself. I think your family was wrong about you."

"You think so?"

"I know so."

Her smile carved warmth into my chest.

We continued to execute the box step, and now we were more relaxed, she seamlessly followed my lead. Every now and again, her hand tightened on my shoulder, especially during the turns. I remained acutely aware of the warmth of her back under my palm and noticed how the skirt swirled around her calves. But we were doing much better.

Carmen clapped her hands to get our attention, and everyone in the class stopped dancing. "Well done. Now, we're going to add music." She floated over to the sound system with an elegant walk. She twisted a knob, and a gentle tune flowed through the speakers, a classical song I didn't recognize but which settled in my muscles.

"Same movements," she instructed. "Remember to let your male partner lead. From the top! One, two, three."

After an awkward start, Tallulah and I waltzed in place, using the music as our guide.

We danced to multiple songs, performing the same steps over and over. With each repetition, the movements became easier and more natural. After a while, I realized I had stopped counting. Carmen wasn't counting either. She moved between us, occasionally repositioning the hand of one student or fixing the posture of another. But ultimately, she allowed us to become one with the music.

Since I wasn't concentrating as hard, I noticed other aspects of Tallulah's appearance. The ring in her nose wasn't a diamond. Upon closer inspection, it appeared to be another type of stone, as it lacked the brilliance of the more expensive gem. I also noticed she bit her bottom lip when she was concentrating, and every now and again she looked up at me and smiled, as if to reassure me that I was doing a good job.

Whenever she did, I wanted to close the distance between us and finish what we had started at the bakery. A problem, I know. A huge problem.

Because Tallulah was the opposite of everything I had convinced myself I needed in my life. I was a planner, but she was someone who went with the flow. She used intuition to make decisions, whereas I relied heavily on data. She was too much like Maria, my ex-wife. Carefree, unconventional, and living by her own set of rules.

Was she really like Maria, though?

Life with my ex had been chaotic, and she tended to make impulsive decisions without considering the consequences. Tallulah, on the other hand, despite her unconventional beliefs, had built a successful business and raised a well-grounded daughter.

She didn't seem as careless as my ex-wife. Her behavior, though different from mine, seemed grounded in intentional actions, and those unconventional beliefs had helped me get the best sleep I'd had in months.

I wanted to know her better, but would it be strange for us to get involved when our kids were marrying each other?

"You're doing it again," Tallulah said.

I blinked. "Doing what?"

"Grinding your teeth and overthinking. A crease appears right above your nose." She lifted her hand from my shoulder and gently tapped the space between my eyebrows. "Right there, when you're thinking hard."

"I think hard a lot."

"Must be exhausting."

"Not really. It's my normal state."

The music ended, and Carmen gave the class a round of applause. "Wonderful job, everyone! I am so very proud of you. Well done. We've come to the end of our first class. The next one is on Thursday, but I recommend you practice at home tomorrow night so you don't lose what you've learned this evening. The more you practice, the easier the steps will become—like second nature. I'll see you all in two days!"

The other couples began gathering their belongings, chatting and laughing. Tallulah and I stepped apart, and longing surged through my chest as I missed the warmth and softness of her body close to mine.

"The class wasn't as terrible as I thought it would be," she said, picking up another one of her colorful bags from against the wall.

"I agree. I'm glad I didn't leave."

She slung the bag across her body and looked at me questioningly. "You were going to leave?"

"Right before you arrived. When I saw you, I changed my mind since I was basically caught."

"Well, I'm glad you stayed."

We said goodnight to the instructor and some of the other students who hung back chatting in the room. Walking down the stairs together, we made our way to the parking lot. Night had fully fallen, and the streetlights cast a golden glow on the cars and buildings around us.

"Thank you," I said.

"For what?" Tallulah asked as we strolled toward our vehicles.

"For not getting angry when I stepped on your foot. For not laughing at me for being incredibly awkward."

"I was laughing on the inside," she said flippantly.

"I figured."

She laughed out loud, the sound as beautiful and engaging as when I had first heard it at the bakery. Something inside me loosened and warmed. Her laughter had been burned into my brain since I first heard it, and I had relived the sound multiple times since then.

She unlocked her car but didn't climb in immediately. Standing beside the door, she held her keys and watched me with an expression I couldn't quite read.

"I heard you were nauseous the day after the bakery incident."

I nodded. "I've never been high before, and after what happened, I don't plan to ever be high again."

"Either you have a low tolerance or you had a bad reaction because you hadn't been exposed to cannabis before."

"I heard you didn't do so well yourself."

"Sadly, I have a low tolerance for weed. I tried it in my twenties and did not fare well. I'm one of those people who have a very intense reaction to it."

"Tough lesson to learn."

"Tell me about it. Well, sir, I enjoyed our dance tonight," she said, speaking in a formal tone.

I followed her lead, speaking in a formal tone as well. "As did I, milady. I'll see you on Thursday."

"So you're definitely coming back?"

"Only if you are." My response seemed to take her by surprise, her mouth falling partially open.

"I do plan to return. I don't want to embarrass my daughter at her wedding."

"I don't want to embarrass my son, but that won't be the reason for my return on Thursday."

"What will be the reason?" Her eyebrows came together.

"My dance partner. So I'll see you on Thursday."

"Yes, you will."

She bit her bottom lip like she had done when we were upstairs dancing and she was concentrating really hard. But this time it wasn't because she was concentrating. She was trying to hide the smile creeping into the corners of her mouth.

"Good night, Jamison."

"Good night, Tallulah." It was the first time I had said her first name out loud, and a spark lit in her eyes. I have to admit, I liked the way her name sounded on my lips.

After she climbed into the car, I backed away and walked to my own vehicle, lighter and more alive than when I had arrived. Rather than pessimistic dread, optimism flooded my veins.

Because despite knowing Tallulah was the opposite of the kind of woman I believed I needed in my life, I looked forward to seeing her again. I looked forward to holding her again.

I looked forward to what was happening between us.

Chapter 17

Tallulah

"Well done!" Carmen clapped, beaming proudly as the music came to an end. "You are ready."

Jamison and I smiled at each other. We, along with the rest of the class, had danced the waltz one final time. Every time he spun me around and I stepped back into his arms, it was like tiptoeing across clouds.

As we said good night to our instructor and the rest of the students, a quiet sadness settled inside me. In a short time, I had come to enjoy our routine and become friendly with my fellow classmates.

Jamison and I were better dancers than when we began, but after tonight, I would no longer be spending time with him.

We filed out of the studio and slowly walked through the parking lot.

"Good night!" everyone called.

We waved, and they waved back.

As he had done three other times before, Jamison escorted me to my vehicle.

"Well, here you are," he announced, stopping beside my car door.

"Yes, here we are," I said, gazing up at him.

Somewhere between missed steps and shared laughs, it dawned on me that he and I weren't as different as I had originally believed. We came in different packaging but shared the same priorities regarding our families, and we were stubbornly devoted to the children we adored. We both had marital scars and carried the invisible weight of marriages that hadn't lasted, making us more careful as a result.

"I hope my son appreciates all the work I put in to make him look good," Jamison said.

"I hope my daughter appreciates all the work I put in too."

An awkward pause rested between us, and we both looked around the parking lot, searching for a topic we could pluck out of the air.

My chest became unbearably heavy, as if someone had set a stone on my sternum. I didn't expect such intense emotions on the last night, as if we were leaving something unfinished. In a way, we were. The night of our first class, he had hinted at his interest, and though he had continued being flirty and friendly, he hadn't made a move on me in the past week.

I wanted him to, and I wanted to spend more time with him.

"Do you have plans for when you leave here?" Jamison asked.

"Nothing special. I'll probably stop by the store on the way home and pick up one of those salad kits so I'll have something to eat tonight. Blossom is at Manuel's working on wedding stuff."

Hands in his pockets, he rocked back on his heels. "I do remember him telling me they were meeting tonight. I believe they finally decided on which food truck they're going to have for the reception."

"Which one?" I asked.

"Both." He grimaced.

"You don't like the food truck idea, do you?"

"No, I don't. I would much prefer a traditional sit-down reception with catering. I offered to help pay for it, but my son refused. They want to do the food truck thing, and he said he could afford the cost. Can you believe those kids?"

"Well..." I hedged, and he stared at me in disbelief.

"Don't tell me you think the food trucks are a good idea?" He sounded appalled.

"Using them has become more popular nowadays, and they're a cost-effective way for couples to cater their weddings. I think it would be kind of fun and represents the special moment when they met."

"I never thought I'd be standing in line at a food truck at a wedding," he grumbled. "But never let it be said that Jamison Harris isn't flexible."

"I'm so proud of you," I teased.

"I've come a long way, haven't I?"

I giggled. "Yes, you have. We both have."

I enjoyed his dry sense of humor, and at random times during the day, I laughed to myself when I remembered one of his sarcastic remarks. We both wanted the best for our kids and were devoted to work that helped people. Could that be why these nights have felt so comfortable? Because we were kindred spirits, in a way? Kindred spirits looking for peace, calm, and no drama.

I was going to miss this strange but easygoing camaraderie that had developed between us.

"Good night!" Carmen strolled by, waving.

"Good night," Jamison and I returned.

Silence fell between us again as we watched her climb into a Mercedes coupe and drive away. We were the last ones in the parking lot, noticeably lingering.

"I should probably go..." I played with the bracelets on my left wrist.

His eyes followed the movement of my fingers. "You know, I was thinking about how our kids insulted us by saying neither one of us could dance."

"I'm still not sure I've forgiven Blossom."

"Because you thought you could dance. I knew I couldn't, but I didn't like Manuel pointing out my flaw. Anyway, I was thinking about what Carmen has said every night. She encouraged us to practice outside of class. Have you been practicing?"

"Not really," I admitted. "Maybe one or two steps here or there, but nothing serious."

"Me either. Practicing without a partner is difficult."

"True," I said, nodding.

"How about we meet up on our own? You could come by my place for dinner, and we could practice our steps to make sure we have them down."

My heart leapt excitedly. "When were you thinking?"

"How about Saturday night?"

"Do you know how to cook?"

"I'm a master griller," he said proudly.

"Oh, really?"

"Oh yeah. People all over Michigan talk about my grilling skills. You haven't heard?"

"No, I haven't," I said, thoroughly amused.

He spread his feet wider and held up his hands. "When I get on the grill, these hands work magic."

Oh my, he looked so damn sexy. I bet his hands were magical.

"I was planning to throw a couple of steaks on the grill

anyway—and before you say a word, I know you don't eat red meat. The steaks will be accompanied by prawns, baked potatoes, and some other kind of vegetable. Call it dinner and dance. Interested?"

I had never seen Jamison like this. His eyes sparkled with a mischievous glint. He obviously loved his plan, and I had to admit the idea of joining him at his place for a home-cooked meal and dancing was enticing.

"Do you need me to bring—"

"Bring only your appetite. I'll have enough food for both of us. You'll actually be doing me a favor. It's hard to cook for one person, and as you already know, I'm very frugal. Most of the time I cook extra so I have enough for dinner the next night. Keeps me from having to cook every night."

"So I'm going to be eating your Sunday night meal?"

"No, because you won't be eating steak, will you?"

"No, I won't."

"So you can enjoy the prawns and the vegetables, and the next day I'll put the extra steak on a salad or chop it up in a sandwich."

A man who cooked and was creative in the kitchen. I was impressed.

"What do you say?" he prodded.

"I would like to see what a master griller—known throughout the state of Michigan—does on the grill. I also like the idea of doing a little dancing. Might as well get in as much practice as we can so we don't embarrass our kids."

His face broke into a smile that made my stomach flip-flop.

"Great. I'll send you my address. What's your number?"

"I gave you my number on a card before, remember? You never entered it in your phone?"

"I... er... lost the card," he said.

Was he lying? I brushed aside my suspicion and repeated my number.

He entered the digits and then sent me a text.

I pulled out my phone and checked the screen. "Got it."

"I'll see you at my place on Saturday," Jamison said after we finalized the time.

I climbed into Orange Julius and watched him walk over to his Lexus. The feeling of a stone sitting on my chest had disappeared and been replaced by warmth and excitement. I didn't want to think too much about what I was feeling, but I couldn't remember the last time I'd looked forward with such anticipation to spending time with a man.

Moments before, I had been bummed he hadn't made a pass at me and that our relationship hadn't progressed past waltzing for an hour each night.

Now, I was going to his home on Saturday. We were going to have dinner. We were going to dance.

Together. Alone. Just the two of us.

Chapter 18

Jamison

I was trying to impress her.

That's why I had invited Tallulah to my condo and offered to grill a meal on my balcony. When I saw her standing outside my condo, her appearance snatched my breath. Instead of her usual colorful ensemble, she was dressed simply, but the effect was still devastatingly impressive.

A blush-colored slip dress skimmed her body, with thin straps resting on the sweep of her shoulders. The fabric caught the light as I ushered her inside, clinging in the right spots to hint at her delicious curves.

She wore her locs sculpted into a high bun, allowing my eyes to feast on the beauty of her eyes, her nose, and the fullness of her lips in a neutral brown color. Large, gold statement earrings brushed her jawline and matched the solitary gold ring on her right hand. Beaded bracelets in different colors were stacked on her wrists, including a rose-colored piece that matched the rose-colored sandals on her feet.

I presented her with a glass of white wine, which she accepted.

"Thank you."

"I hope you like cilantro," I said.

"Love it. I love all kinds of herbs."

"Perfect. Dinner will be ready soon."

She followed me out to the balcony where I had the grill set up and two ribeyes sizzling on the hot grates. She sat in one of the lounge chairs while I tended to the food.

"The city sounds far away. It's nice up here," Tallulah commented.

"I agree. We currently have contractors working on the rooftop to turn it into a space we can all use. Owners without balconies are especially looking forward to having the outdoor space."

She groaned softly. "I bet the president of your association loves organizing that project."

"Guess who's the president of the association," I said.

Her eyes widened. "Don't tell me it's you," she said, a burst of laughter spilling from her throat.

I loved the sound of her laughter and temporarily forgot to respond. When I first saw her at Knife & Fork, I noticed her attractiveness, but getting to know her and seeing her relaxed and happy made her more than attractive. She was one of the most beautiful women I had ever seen.

"You guessed right," I finally said.

"You couldn't help yourself, could you?" she asked with amusement.

"Planning is in my blood." I placed broccolini on the grill. "What did you tell Blossom you were doing tonight?"

"I didn't have to tell her anything. She's been MIA the past few days, spending all her time at your son's place. She sent a text letting me know she'll be back tonight, and I told her that depending on what time she came home, I might be out having dinner, but I'd see her later."

She paused, playing with a chunky aqua-blue bracelet. "I take yoga on Monday nights at the wellness center. I like the camaraderie, and it keeps me mindful of my form and so on. But most of the time I do yoga and meditation at home. I turned an extra bedroom into an exercise studio and meditation room. Blossom uses it too, and sometimes we exercise together. Not as much as we used to since we both have our own lives now."

I heard the sadness in her voice. "You miss those times with her."

"I do. I selfishly believed when she returned from college we'd go back to life as usual."

"I can relate," I said, easing the steaks onto a plate and covering them with foil. "Manuel and I used to go to the gym together. Then when he went off to college, I lost my gym buddy. Now that he's back, it's obvious he no longer wants to hang with his old man. He has his own friends, younger guys he goes to the gym with now. We do very little together anymore."

"What else did you used to do together?" Tallulah asked, taking a sip of wine.

"Not as much as I'd like, to be honest. I allowed work to be more of a priority than it should've been."

"In what way?"

"You turned your spare bedroom into an exercise studio and meditation room. I turned mine into a home office so I could work from home."

"The one thing my ex-husband and I always agreed on was keeping work out of our house. I was adamant about that, and he agreed. The separation was also a priority when I opened Simply Well. I didn't want to disturb the energy in my home—and don't you *dare* make a smart remark." She pointed a finger at me.

"Like what?" I asked innocently.

"Like you doubt the concept of energy."

"I believe that you believe it," I said carefully, not wishing to offend her. Funny how my attitude had changed. I hadn't given a damn about offending her the first time we met.

She eyed me with a healthy dose of skepticism. "I deal with the fears and worries of my customers all day. When I'm at home, I want a clear separation so I can reset and recharge. Bringing work home means my body and mind never get the message that it's time to rest."

Though I probably wouldn't use the word energy, what she said made sense.

"So my office is at the store," Tallulah continued. "Where I do paperwork and inventory and all the tasks required to run my business. When my husband moved away, the nights I had to work late, Blossom would do her homework in the office with me or at the counter out front. Only recently have I started doing any work at home, and I don't consider it work. I make kombucha. It's really more of a hobby. I made it for myself and then started making extra to sell in the store."

"Then it took off," I surmised.

"Then it took off," she confirmed. "I could probably sell more than I do since I sell out every week, but I'm satisfied with this pace. Since I make a small batch, I can do it out of my home kitchen. If I sold more, I'd have to get a commercial kitchen, and I'm not interested in going that route. At least not at the moment."

"When you're ready to expand, let me know. I'll help you with the numbers."

"How much would your assistance cost?"

"Nothing. We're going to be family soon, so consider it a favor. Besides, I owe you since I've been having some of the best sleep of my life."

We were both quiet for a while as I added the prawns to the

grill. They sizzled, joining the chorus of sound from the rest of the cooking food and the noise from the street below.

"Why did you choose to live here? It's nice, but you seem like the type who would have a big house and a three-car garage on the edge of town."

"You couldn't be more wrong. I've never wanted all that because it's not practical. I bought this place after my wife and I divorced, but I did have the big house with the three-car garage on the edge of town."

"She wanted those things, not you," Tallulah guessed.

I nodded. "Despite giving her what she wanted, Maria—my ex-wife—wasn't happy. She didn't like the budget I set for the household. She called me a tightwad." I frowned. Since when did being smart about money become a bad thing?

"Are you a tightwad?" Tallulah asked.

"I prefer the word frugal."

"There must be a reason for your behavior. You didn't wake up one morning and decide to create a budget for your household and expect your wife to stick to it."

"I've always been this way. I grew up pretty poor. My parents had six kids when they probably should've had one or none. We never had much, and then they took in two of my cousins because my aunt and uncle were unable to take care of them. Long story involving substance abuse and all it entails. Anyway, they were barely able to provide for six of us, and now there were two more mouths to feed and bodies to clothe."

"Sounds rough." Tallulah's eyes filled with sympathy.

"You have no idea. I can't say I ever went hungry, but I did grow tired of rice and beans. And you would not believe the many ways you can cook cabbage." We both had a laugh. "We never threw anything away, and my siblings and I shared clothes. Clothes handed down from folks at church or clothes my parents had purchased at Goodwill or yard sales for pennies on the dollar. They were patched and recycled between all of us. As you can imagine, we were not the popular kids in school and were teased mercilessly."

I shifted the vegetables and prawns onto a platter. "When I became an adult, I promised myself I would do things differently. I paid my way through school, working full-time while going to school full-time. I made sure I picked a major that would make me money, determined not to want for anything again. When I met Maria, deep down I knew we were incompatible, but she was so different. So full of light, and our chemistry was off the charts. I overlooked our differences and believed our relationship would work because we loved each other."

"Famous last words," Tallulah muttered.

"Yeah. Our differences became magnified after we got married, and it became clear we should've had more in-depth conversations. She wanted a big family, like the one she was a part of. At least four kids, she said."

"And how many did you want?"

"Two, but only if we could afford them. After we had Manuel, she kept talking about having more kids, and I showed her in the budget where that wasn't possible."

Tallulah gasped. "Not the budget again. Tell me you didn't whip out a budget and tell your wife you couldn't have more children."

"Did you forget what I said about how I grew up? She was not happy."

"Do you regret not having more children?"

"I do sometimes. I would've liked to have had two kids. A girl would've been nice. But lucky me, I'll have one, with Blossom coming into our lives."

I could see she was pleased by my comment, which I sincerely meant. I was looking forward to having her daughter as a member of our family. Over the past few weeks, I had gotten to know her, and she truly was a special young woman. I understood why my son was attracted to her. Not only because of her outer appearance, but she also had an inner beauty. She was kind and smart and loved Manuel.

Despite what I thought about her job prospects initially, she was hunting for a job on a regular basis, determined to find a career in her field. They would be fine on a personal level, as well as financially, which had been a major concern of mine. She would be a good partner for him.

What more could a parent ask for in their child's future spouse?

Chapter 19

Tallulah

I sat down at the table, impressed with the spread before me. Jamison had outdone himself. I popped one of the prawns in my mouth when his back was turned, and it was grilled to perfection and very flavorful with his cilantro sauce. I'd have to find a way to get the recipe out of him.

We ate outside on the balcony. Below us, the city of Ellington was quiet yet busy. Quieter than a place like New York, but alive with the sounds of the night—a siren wailing in the distance, the low rush of passing cars, and laughter drifting up from the sidewalk.

Jamison was dressed in jeans and a soft gray Henley, both of which looked fantastic on him, the shirt molding to his muscular torso and the denim hugging his firm legs. He drank beer while I had water to accompany my second glass of wine. We ate in silence for a few minutes before he finally looked at me.

"Well?"

I finished chewing a grilled baby corn. "I'm sorry, I was

enjoying the food so much I forgot to tell you how good it is. Absolutely delicious!" I said enthusiastically.

He grinned. "Thank you."

"You're welcome. Did you cook like this when you were married?"

"I've been cooking like this since high school. I was the second oldest, so I helped take care of the younger ones. My older sister Lori, by the way, ended up not having children of her own. She said she had raised seven kids already and was done."

"Is Lori married?" I took a sip of water.

He nodded as he chewed a piece of steak. "She found someone she was compatible with. Her husband is a great guy and didn't want kids either."

"Smart Lori."

"Very."

"So what finally ended your marriage, if you don't mind my asking? Was it the financial incompatibility?"

He stopped eating, a pained expression crossing his face. "I wish. If our problems had remained financial, we could have worked through them. Maria had an affair."

I involuntarily gasped, hoping I hadn't dredged up painful memories. "I'm sorry."

He shrugged. "We were having problems, but cheating certainly didn't help. We couldn't come back from that."

He said *we*, but he probably really meant *he* couldn't forgive her for that final betrayal.

"They didn't last. She had several more relationships before marrying an accountant and having two kids."

"You ever thought about getting married again?"

"It has crossed my mind. What about you?"

I paused, not because I didn't know the answer but because

I had never said my thoughts out loud to another person. "I would like to get married again. I like having a partner and someone to do activities with. Someone to talk to." I pushed the broccolini around on my plate. "But next time, I'm going to make sure we're compatible. I'm not making the same mistake twice."

Slowly, he nodded, studying me in silence. "Why did you and your husband end up getting divorced?"

"How much time do you have?"

"As much as you need to tell the story."

"I'll keep it short," I promised. "Karl—that's my husband's name—and I were having problems, like you and Maria. Then one day he told me he wasn't happy and wanted a divorce."

"Was there someone else?"

I shook my head, stabbing a prawn with my fork. "He just didn't want me anymore."

The truth had been brutally painful to digest. I'm not sure which was worse: losing your spouse because of someone else or losing them because they didn't want you.

"I'm sorry. He was a fool."

"You think so?" I asked, appreciative of his attempt to make me feel better.

"I know so," he said with surprising intensity, his eyes never leaving mine.

The spark—whatever you want to call it—returned. Stronger. More of a charge reaching across the table.

It didn't help that he looked extra appealing tonight in his casual clothes, the sleeves of the Henley shoved up to his elbows to showcase strong forearms covered in fine hairs. He'd had a haircut too, revealing more of his distinguishing gray hairs.

I glanced down at my plate to regain my bearings. "Karl remarried, and Blossom has two younger sisters. She's not very close with them because of the distance and the age difference, but she has continued to have a good relationship with her father, which I appreciate. I was worried our split would mean losing her relationship with him, but that never happened."

After we finished dinner, I helped Jamison clean up and wash the dishes. Then we lingered outside for a bit, our arms resting on the metal railing as we overlooked the city. We talked some more and shared stories about our marriages. Not as a way to complain or bash our exes, but to point out the mistakes that were made and how we had bounced back from them.

He told me that he and Maria got along much better now, proof—in his opinion—they never should have married in the first place. I admitted my relationship with Karl hadn't improved since our divorce, and we were simply cordial to each other.

We exchanged funny workplace stories and admitted we couldn't imagine doing any other work than what we did on a daily basis.

"Is that your car down there?" Jamison asked, pointing into the parking lot.

"Yes, that's Orange Julius."

"You named your car?"

"I had to. There's so much history riding on those tires, it's practically part of the family. Both of my parents were teachers. My mother taught math and my father was an art teacher, so we always had the summers free, and the year I turned thirteen, they took us on our first road trip. From then on, we traveled the whole summer, every year. We slept and ate in the bus. The first time I saw the Pacific Ocean was from the back of that bus."

"Were your parents hippies?" Jamison asked, looking handsome with a soft smile on his face.

"Hippie adjacent. My middle name is Flower, by the way."

"You're kidding."

"No," I shook my head, laughing. "Tallulah Flower Washington."

"It suits you."

"You think so?"

His eyes skimmed my appearance, and heat coated my skin. "Definitely."

We eventually moved into the living room, where Jamison pushed the coffee table out of the way to make room for us to dance.

"We might as well get comfortable," he said, removing his shoes.

"Oh, I like this." I slipped off my sandals.

"I figured you would."

I rested my hands on my hips. "What does that mean?"

"You seem like the type who'd walk around barefoot if it weren't socially taboo."

"You know me too well."

We both laughed.

He turned on the music, and all of a sudden, the mood in the room changed. It was the same type of song we had danced to in the studio, but this time was different. We weren't surrounded by other students and didn't have Carmen's watchful eyes on us or the bright lights shining down from the ceiling. Instead, we were alone in his condo with only the muted glow of two lamps in the room.

Jamison extended a hand. "Ready?"

I stepped closer, my bare feet silent on the cool hardwood floor. The second we touched, I experienced the same electric awareness that had been building between us during every dance lesson and each time our gazes held for a beat too long.

His firm hand settled against my back, the warmth of his palm seeping into my skin through the soft fabric of my dress. I placed my hand on his strong shoulder and met his eyes, my back automatically straightening into the precise posture Carmen had drilled into me, though I longed to lean closer.

We began to move. "One, two, three," Jamison murmured.

Our bodies found the rhythm, and we danced with the ease earned from doing the same steps repeatedly. Jamison led with confidence, no longer tentative or uncomfortable, and I followed instinctively and without hesitation.

He spun me out and then pulled me in closer than necessary before we separated again, gliding through the movements we had rehearsed dozens of times. Each spin out and reel in brought us closer, and when his hand slid lower on my back, my breath caught. He held me against him, our faces mere inches apart. Then his gaze dropped to my lips.

"Tallulah." My name was a rough sound in his throat.

The music continued, but we had stopped moving. We stood still, both of us breathing hard, as if we'd just finished running the Ellington Memorial Day Marathon. His hands cupped my face, one thumb tracing my cheekbone with devastating gentleness.

He looked down at me with heavy-lidded eyes. "When I said your husband was a fool, I wasn't just talking. I meant it."

He dipped his head, and I held my breath. He paused, his eyes searching mine.

"Do you want me to stop?" he whispered.

I gave my answer when I lifted onto my toes.

The kiss started softly, tentatively, as if we were asking a question. His lips brushed mine once, twice, testing my response. I answered by threading my fingers through his hair, pulling him closer.

My actions unleashed something in him, and the kiss deepened, turned hungry. His arm clamped around my waist, and he lifted me to the tips of my toes, crushing my body into his as he angled his mouth over mine. I tasted the tang of beer on his lips and pulled him closer, pushing my tongue into his mouth to explore more deeply.

I touched him everywhere I could—sliding my hands from his hair to his shoulders, down his torso and up his back—taking my pleasure in learning the solid warmth of his body. He made a sound low in his throat—half groan, half surrender—and walked me backward until I hit the wall. He cradled the back of my head, kissing me with more demand, with more passion.

The classical music continued to play, background noise completely ignored as his mouth trailed a fiery path from my lips to my jaw and down the column of my neck. Tilting back my head, I gave him full access and felt him smile against my skin before he kissed the sensitive spot behind my ear.

"Should we talk about this?" he asked huskily, gripping my ass with both hands.

"Later," I panted, pulling his mouth back to mine.

"Much later," he whispered against my lips.

He kissed me again, thoroughly and hard, as if he'd been waiting weeks to do so.

Maybe he had—just like I had been.

Chapter 20

Tallulah

Jamison pulled back from the kiss, breathing hard, his forehead resting against mine. "Bedroom?"

The gutturally spoken word carried the weight of every single thought we hadn't spoken out loud.

I nodded, not trusting my ability to speak.

He gripped my hand and led the way down the hallway to his bedroom. Fleetingly, I noticed it was neat and organized with minimal furniture and a king bed with white sheets and a charcoal gray blanket. But the way he looked at me was far more important.

He reached for me, and I stepped into his arms, his hands settling on my waist and drawing me in. His hard erection pressed against my lower abdomen, and I took a shaky, excited breath.

"Are you sure?" Jamison asked quietly.

"Stop overthinking."

His mouth briefly curled upward, and then he began to undress me without hesitation. It was as if I had fired the starting gun at a race, and he was off and running.

My dress slid to the floor in a heap at my feet, and since I wasn't wearing a bra, the only other garment that needed removing was my panties. I'd come prepared tonight. Instead of sensible cotton, I was wearing a lacy, high-waisted number that flattered my shape and barely covered my ass. It landed on the floor at my feet too, and then he removed my bangles and placed them on the table beside the bed. Several fell to the floor, but we ignored them, focused solely on each other.

"My turn to undress you," I said softly, my voice breathless with anticipation.

I grasped the hem of his Henley and slipped it over his head. I knew the man had a nice body, but seeing him half naked was impressive. Lean and solid, he had the kind of build that came from disciplined workouts.

I eagerly palmed his chest, moving my hands over the dark hair sprinkled on his warm skin. Then I slid my hands lower to unhook his jeans.

"Your body..." I breathed, shaking my head. "I can't wait to see all of it."

When he stepped out of his pants, I bit my bottom lip, awed by the sight of his powerful thighs and his very impressive erection.

Jamison lifted my hand and kissed the inside of my wrist, sucking the flesh as he climbed toward my elbow. My pulse hammered at the tender eroticism of the gesture.

Then his mouth captured mine again, and he crushed me against him with pure emotion and unrestrained desire. He tormented me with his teeth and tongue, stroking the inside of my mouth and nipping at my lips.

With my breasts pressed against his chest, the tingle of the short hairs added another layer of sensation that made me whimper with pleasure.

We tumbled onto the bed, arms and legs wrapping around each other, hips grinding as we strained to get closer. He plundered my lips with hungry kisses before dragging his mouth lower to assail my throat with the same delicious urgency. Arching my head back, I savored the torture and wanted more.

His mouth on my breast made me gasp, made my belly quiver and my loins ache for his possession. He sucked my nipples until I groaned and undulated restlessly beneath him, twisting on the linens. I wanted to retreat while simultaneously pushing my flesh deeper into his mouth so his stiff tongue could flit against the turgid peak.

When he went lower, my teeth sank into my lip again, and I inhaled a deep breath as he draped my legs over his shoulders. I opened myself wide and lifted my hips for his mouth, desperate for him to take his fill. And he did. Oh, how he did, sucking, tonguing me, driving me mad until my body trembled with the shock of an eye-crossing orgasm. The sounds of my hoarse cries filled the room as he relentlessly devoured me, his groans of satisfaction adding to the carnal intimacy that left me gasping and trembling, hardly able to breathe as I completely lost control.

"Goddamn delicious." The words came out as a growl as he made his way back up my body.

He kissed my neck and my jaw. "What is that scent you're wearing? It drives me crazy."

"Body butter. I make it myself from vanilla and honey."

"I love it."

I reached for him, taking his hard length in my hand and stroking until I saw in his eyes that his control was fraying.

"I need you. I need you now," he said huskily.

He yanked the drawer open in the nightstand beside the bed and removed a condom. He rolled it on and then settled between my thighs. "I want to lose myself inside you," he said with a husky groan.

I lifted both my legs around his waist and crossed them above his ass. Lust flared in his eyes as the tip of his hard length pushed at my entrance.

He plunged into my body, and I gasped out loud, angling my hips higher. "Yes, just like that..."

"Tallulah," he gritted out, his face contorted into a mask of passion.

"Don't hold back," I urged.

We locked gazes, his light eyes darkening as he withdrew and then plunged right back into me again. Dominant. Rocking my body beneath his. With each thrust, pleasure shot through me. Each time he buried himself to the hilt, I squeezed my feminine muscles, dragging a sound of pure pleasure from deep inside his chest.

Our sensually rough lovemaking was immensely satisfying, and each time we changed positions, I marveled at his stamina and how he commanded my body, pushing me past thought into pure, helpless sensation.

He entered me from the side, his hands squeezing my breasts and making my core drip and ache as his name spilled from my lips. He pushed me to my knees and entered me from behind, forcing my back into an arch and my face into the pillow. As my carefully coiffed hair cascaded onto the white sheets, he held me down with a well-placed hand at the back of my neck. His hips slammed against my ass, dragging me under, narrowing our world to where our bodies were joined.

In the final position, he pushed me onto my back again, and that's when I gripped him—panting, begging, pleading for more.

His rhythm never faltered. He moved with precision,

denying his own release while giving me multiple orgasms. And right when I was certain I would die from ecstasy, he cupped my buttocks and drove in deep, whispering my name into the side of my neck, painting my skin with the warmth of his breath.

His fingers squeezed my cheeks, and he let out a sound like a wounded animal as his own release erupted. With him trapped between my thighs, I absorbed every convulsion. My name on his lips was half exclamation, half surrender, and he collapsed on top of me, his body finally claiming the bliss he had given me so freely.

Moments later, both of us breathing hard, he slowly slid his hands from beneath me, and I let my legs go lax.

Jamison looked down at me. "That was..."

He seemed to lose the words he was about to speak. But I understood. He didn't need to finish the sentence.

"Yeah. I agree."

He rolled off me and went into the bathroom to dispose of the condom. When he returned, I had slipped under the covers, and he joined me, pulling me into his arms.

Jamison traced a lazy pattern on my back. "You have no idea how long I've been wanting to see your hair spread out across my pillows like this." He wound one of my locks around his finger.

"How long?"

"From when I came to your store to apologize."

"You were checking me out way back then?"

"Oh yeah," he said without shame.

"Want to know something?"

"What?"

"I was checking you out then too."

He brought his lips to mine in a searing kiss.

I stroked his prominent jawline and slid my fingers into his hair, purring my satisfaction. I caressed his hips, his buttocks, and licked his chin.

We had crossed the line tonight, and I had no idea what would happen next, but I was determined to live in this moment.

To enjoy every second in his arms for the rest of the night.

Chapter 21

Tallulah

I quietly entered my house and eased the door shut.

I felt ridiculous—a forty-seven-year-old woman sneaking into my own home like a teenager after curfew, but I didn't want to wake Blossom and also didn't want to have a conversation about where I had been, what I had been doing, and with whom.

My lips were still swollen from Jamison's kisses, and my skin was extremely sensitive, as if each nerve ending was humming. If I focused too much on the way he had looked at me before I left—his light eyes filled with longing, as if he didn't want me to go—I'd start blushing.

I crept through the dark living room, cursing the old squeaky floorboards as I made my way toward the back.

Had I really slept with Jamison? It seemed like a reckless thing to do, but I had thoroughly enjoyed myself. He was a skilled lover. The control and precision he applied to spreadsheets and financial projections—or whatever he did at the bank—were apparently transferable to the bedroom.

Very transferable.

I bit my lip to keep from smiling like an idiot in the darkness.

As I neared Blossom's bedroom, her door flew open, and I froze. In the dim light, I saw my daughter dressed in pajamas, rubbing sleep from her eyes.

"Mom, what are you doing coming home so late?"

"Sorry. Did I wake you?" I purposely avoided answering the question and kept my face neutral.

"Honestly, I couldn't sleep. You didn't respond to any of my texts."

"I'm sorry. I missed your messages."

I even looked at my phone since I left Jamison's. I'd been in my own world, high off sex with a buttoned-up banker who wasn't so buttoned-up in private.

Focus, Tallulah.

"You could've called and told me you'd be coming home late. I was worried," Blossom said.

What was happening here? She was acting like a parent and treating me like a child. I was amused and slightly mortified by the role reversal.

"I'll be sure to respond next time. I'll see you in the morning," I said, trying to brush by her.

Please let this be over so I can escape to my room and continue processing what happened, I thought.

"Mom, you didn't answer my question. What were you doing out so late?" Frowning, she stared at me. "Were you having sex?"

Why did she sound alarmed? How did she think she came into this world?

And what the heck made her jump to that conclusion? Could she smell the sex on me? Was it somehow written on my face? Did I have a post-coital glow going on in the dimly lit hallway?

"Go to bed, Blossom," I said dismissively. "We'll talk in the morning. I'm tired, okay?" This time I didn't stick around. I took off toward my room.

"Are you tired from having sex?" This time, Blossom's voice was high-pitched, almost like a screech.

Good grief, this child. I was *not* having this conversation with her. I opened my door and locked it with a satisfying click.

"Mom! I'm not done talking to you!" Blossom wiggled the doorknob and rapped her knuckles against the door.

Sighing, I stood in the middle of my dark room, contemplating what to do next. I really didn't want to have a conversation with my daughter about having sex with her future father-in-law. Not tonight. Not tomorrow. Not ever.

So I ignored her calls from the other side of the door, her constant knocking, and removed my phone from my purse and plugged it into the outlet next to my bed.

"Mom, stop ignoring me. You're being rude!" Blossom accused.

I considered responding but then decided against it. Silence was the best recourse at the moment. Besides, what was I supposed to tell her?

"You know how you wanted me and Jamison to get along? Well, we get along great now. Especially horizontally." Wink, wink.

Or better yet, I could say something like, "Well, my love, I had an amazing night with Manuel's father. We had sex—first on his bed and then I straddled him on the chair in his bedroom and rode him like a horse."

I seriously doubted she wanted to hear the details.

I went into the bathroom, stripped off my clothes, and stepped into the shower. Lifting my face into the warm, soothing spray, I relived Jamison's hands on my body. The way he traced my curves, not only with his fingers but with his lips and tongue. The way he'd whispered my name like a prayer, and when his control finally snapped... I shivered. He'd been like an animal—a sensually demanding animal.

I laughed to myself, shaking my head. I needed to focus on actually washing my body instead of standing under the spray, grinning like a fool.

When I finally stepped out of the shower, feeling refreshed and clean, Blossom was no longer knocking. She must've gotten tired and gone back to her room. Guilt nudged my conscience for ignoring her, but talking could wait until the morning.

Jamison and I didn't discuss what happened, but I was fairly certain he was of the same mind: this wasn't something we should share with our kids.

At least not yet. Maybe not ever. Sleeping together was complicated enough without adding our children's opinions into the mix.

I rubbed my vanilla and honey body butter all over my skin, smiling when I remembered how much Jamison said he enjoyed the scent. Then I slipped on a sheer nightgown. Tonight, it felt especially sensual against my skin after my night with Jamison, the silky fabric sliding over my thighs reminding me of his touch.

Was he thinking about me too, or was this a slam-bam-thank-you-ma'am type of deal?

I sobered a little.

What if I were mooning over a man who had already moved on mentally, slotting the evening under "a pleasant hookup," and then going about his life as if nothing happened?

"Do not get attached," I muttered to myself as I gathered my hair into a high ponytail. I then tied a blue and gold scarf turban style around my head.

Getting attached to Jamison Harris would be a bad move.

The sex had been amazing. Mind-blowing. But he hadn't made any mention of us seeing each other again.

My phone buzzed. Already under the covers, I leaned over to check the screen and saw a missed call from Jamison, which he had followed up with a text.

My heart did an Olympic-worthy somersault.

So much for not getting attached.

Jamison: I know I'm not supposed to be on my phone in bed, but I had to make sure you got home safely.

How sweet of him.

Me: Made it home fine. Currently in bed right now, about to go to sleep. Blossom gave me the third degree for coming in late.

I hit send before I suffered from Jamison-type overthinking.

Jamison: Uh oh. Are you in trouble?

I could practically hear the laughter in his text.

Me: I'm grown.

Jamison: So should I assume you're not going to tell her what happened tonight?

I stared at the screen, unsure how to respond. I hadn't planned to tell my daughter, but was he suggesting I should? Or was he hoping I wouldn't?

Instead of answering, I posed my own question: Are you telling Manuel?

He didn't respond right away, probably thinking about the answer the same way I had been.

The three dots appeared, then disappeared, then appeared again. I held my breath.

Jamison: I don't have plans to.

Relief flooded through me, maybe because I wasn't sure where our "relationship" was going.

Me: I don't plan to tell Blossom.

Jamison: Seems we're in agreement.

Me: Yes.

We were good at being in agreement when we were alone, apparently. Very good.

Jamison: I had a great time tonight. I'm not just talking about, you know.

I smiled.

Me: I did too.

The night had been special for many reasons, and it was the best night I'd had in a long time. Dinner, dancing, and deep conversations with laughter sprinkled in. I laughed at his jokes, and he laughed at mine, particularly my story about the time I had accidentally ordered five thousand ginseng tinctures instead of fifty. An absolute nightmare, but I didn't mind sharing my mistakes with him.

Jamison: Good night.

Me: Good night.

I replaced my phone on the nightstand and stared up at the fan above my bed.

Moving forward, were we going to pretend tonight didn't happen and go back to being cordial acquaintances whose children were getting married? Could we? More importantly—did I want to?

Turning onto my side, I twisted into a more comfortable position and closed my eyes.

There was no point in dwelling on possibilities. I couldn't predict the future, so I simply had to wait and see what the universe had in store for us. For tonight, I'd hold onto the memory of Jamison's hands on my body, the look of adoration in his gray eyes, his mouth on mine, and the husky way he said my name, as if I were extremely special.

I hadn't felt special in a long time, so long I had forgotten the quiet pleasure of it. I intended to savor this feeling.

For now.

Chapter 22

Tallulah

I scrolled through the slides of my presentation on the computer as I stood behind the counter at work. Tyler, Leslie, and I had a meeting with the landlord, and they had elected me to take the lead.

Yay.

I had assumed Tyler would jump at the chance to be the leader since he had initially organized our first business owners' meeting. Unfortunately, he seemed intimidated by the idea of speaking to the landlord on behalf of the group, so I guess it was going to be me.

The door opened, temporarily letting in the sounds from the plaza outside. I looked up and froze.

Jamison stood in the doorway in a charcoal suit, holding a small paper sack in one hand. I didn't know whether to be happy or upset.

Four days had passed.

Four days since I left his condo in the middle of the night, thoroughly satisfied and wondering what would happen next.

Four days since we communicated by text.

Four days of me not obsessing over whether sleeping with him had been a mistake because I don't obsess. I go with the flow. Yeah, right.

"Hello, Jamison," I said, proud that my voice came out steady and warm. "What are you doing here?"

He strolled over and placed the bag on the counter. "You left something at my place."

I opened the sack, suspecting I already knew what was inside. One of my bangles had been missing since my night at his condo. I knew for certain I had been wearing it, so I must have lost it at his place, but I had hesitated to reach out.

I lifted out my aqua blue bangle and slipped it onto my wrist with the multicolored collection I was wearing. "Thank you. You didn't have to come all the way here to drop this off. You could've m–"

"Mailed it. I know. Or sent it through Blossom."

I looked up at him with renewed interest. "But you didn't."

"No."

We eyed each other across the counter as if we were alone, though there were two people browsing inside the store. My mind immediately went to the hours we had spent together wearing significantly fewer clothes and how he had made me throb and ache and surrender to his will.

Jamison watched my mouth in the same way he had right before he kissed me in his living room.

One of us had to say something, so I did. "How have you been?"

"Busy. You?"

"Same."

This was ridiculous. We were seasoned adults, not teenagers or young twenty-somethings. We had sex—enthusiastically—and it was extremely satisfying, and now we couldn't talk, behaving like awkward acquaintances.

"Tallulah—"

"Jamison—"

We spoke at the same time and stopped at the same time. He gestured for me to continue.

"I wanted to say that we don't have to be weird about what happened."

"Agreed. We had sex."

"Yes."

He tapped his finger on the counter. "I just wanted to come by and drop off the bracelet. I didn't want you to be looking for it."

"I appreciate your thoughtfulness."

He ran his fingers through his hair, a gesture I was beginning to recognize meant he was uncomfortable or unsure of himself.

He lowered his voice. "Look, I know we didn't discuss what will happen next, and the timing of us meeting and hooking up is complicated by our kids planning a wedding—"

The door opened again, and we both turned our heads. Blossom walked in with her laptop bag over one shoulder. She stopped short when she saw Jamison, eyebrows lifting in surprise.

"Hi, Mr. Harris." Her eyes darted between us. "What are you doing here?"

"I was..."

"He had questions about which kinds of teas would be beneficial for him to drink," I said, proud of myself for saving him, not proud of lying.

Blossom frowned. "Really? Manuel told me once that you didn't like tea. You said it was for people whose taste buds couldn't appreciate coffee."

"My son tends to exaggerate," Jamison said with an embarrassed laugh.

"He said if you had a choice, you'd inject coffee into your veins and toss all the tea into the sea like they did at the Boston Tea Party."

I stared at Jamison. Why in the world did he hate tea so much?

"Again, a bit of an exaggeration," Jamison said.

"But didn't you—"

"Blossom," I said, interrupting to save him.

She had the same analytical mind as her father and wouldn't stop until Jamison's answer coincided with what Manuel had told her about his father. I also needed to speak up since I was the one who had come up with what I thought was the perfect lie. I had no idea I was dealing with an anti-tea activist.

"He's slowly exploring options and learning about the health benefits. What are *you* doing here?" I asked my daughter.

"I was at the library doing research and came by to see if you had anything to eat so I wouldn't have to drive all the way home."

To get out of the house, she had been going to the library while job hunting online. Fortunately for me, she had not pushed for more information after I came home late on Saturday night. She did watch me with suspicion as we ate breakfast on Sunday but never broached the topic of my alleged sexual exploits.

"I have pasta salad and half a tomato sandwich in the little refrigerator in the break room. You can have both," I said.

"Cool. Thanks."

She went to the back, leaving Jamison and me alone again. Unfortunately, one of the customers chose the same moment to approach. Jamison stepped aside so the man could place his selections on the counter. I quickly rang him up, and he left.

Jamison opened his mouth to speak, but Blossom emerged from the back with the containers of food. "I'm going back to the library," she announced, pulling my last kombucha from the small refrigerator. She paused, eyes sweeping over the two of us. "You know, Manuel also mentioned you've been in a really good mood lately. Whistling at work, that kind of thing. I guess getting enough sleep has really helped, hasn't it?"

"Certainly has," Jamison confirmed.

"I told you my mom was good," Blossom said.

"She certainly knows her stuff." Blossom had no idea, but he was speaking with double entendre, which made my cheeks burn.

"See you later, Mom." Blossom waved as she headed toward the door.

"Bye, my love."

The door shut quietly behind her.

"Do you think she knows?" Jamison asked in a lowered voice.

"No. She suspects I was with someone on Saturday night, but she has no idea it was you. She's too preoccupied with job hunting, wedding plans, and Manuel. Keeping what happened to ourselves was the right decision, at least for now."

"Agreed." He fell quiet for a moment. "When I walked in, you were frowning. Is everything all right?"

Knowing he recognized my distress made warmth unfurl in my chest. "Nothing I can't handle."

"Tallulah," he chided.

"No, really. It's a business-related issue I'm working on," I said dismissively.

"What kind of business issue?" Concern filled his voice.

I hesitated, unsure if I wanted to burden him with my problem. "In a couple of days, I and two other business owners in the building will have a meeting with the new landlord to discuss our concerns. We were elected by the other tenants to be the points of contact."

"What concerns do you have?" Jamison asked.

"We're worried about getting pushed out, the way the company pushed out tenants when they bought other buildings. I wanted to have a strong showing, with the names of all the tenants on the letter we're going to present to the landlord, but half of the business owners didn't sign the darn thing. They're worried about backlash, which is extremely frustrating."

"Can you reschedule to try to get more signatures?"

I shook my head. "I don't know if a delay will do any good. Besides, the landlord gave us one date and made sure we understood he was doing us a favor. He has a very packed schedule, et cetera, et cetera. He's flying out of town this weekend and will be gone until Wednesday of next week, so we couldn't even push the meeting forward a few days if we wanted to." I leaned against the counter, the weight of the meeting settling between my shoulder blades like a muscle ache. "I hope he listens to us. If they drastically increase the rent, most of us won't be able to stay."

"I had no idea you were dealing with this."

"Yeah. Wish us luck," I said, laughing without humor.

His expression turned thoughtful, the line appearing between his eyebrows, which meant he was processing and thinking deeply about what I had told him.

"Do you feel prepared for the meeting? What's his name, by the way?"

"Freedom Capital Real Estate is the company, and Jason Ochoa is the landlord and the person we've been talking to. I'm as prepared as I can be. We have an organized, visually attractive presentation, and I'll be leading the meeting."

"I'm sure you'll do an excellent job," Jamison said. "Take

your time, present your case, and show Mr. Ochoa why it's beneficial to have all of you stay. He's not going to be concerned about you. You have to show him how half the businesses leaving will hurt him, even if it's what the company has done in the past. Turnover is costly."

"I'll be sure to convey the message. You were about to say something before Blossom came in...?"

He tapped the counter. "I forgot what I was about to say, so it wasn't very important."

His answer disappointed me. I didn't believe he had forgotten.

"You have more pressing issues to deal with," Jamison continued. "If you need help with your presentation, let me know."

"I will," I said. My second lie of the day.

I didn't feel comfortable enough in our newfound closeness to ask for his assistance. Besides, we didn't have much time. The meeting was in two days.

"Let me know how the meeting goes."

"I will," I said again. My third lie of the day.

Jamison left soon after, leaving bitter disappointment in his wake. I didn't doubt the attraction we had for each other. After all, we'd spent a wonderful night together and had sex twice. I can't remember the last time I orgasmed that many times in one night. The last time had probably been with my ex-husband, more than ten years ago.

While I didn't doubt the attraction and chemistry between me and Jamison, he was hesitating, and so was I. Neither of us wanted to be the first to put ourselves out there, and I understood why. Based on our conversations, we were both once again attracted to someone different than ourselves, which hadn't worked out in our first marriages.

"Can I help you find anything?" I called to the remaining customer.

"I'm just browsing. Are these part of the sale?" She held up a tincture.

"Yes. Twenty-five percent off."

"Thanks." She placed two in the basket on her arm.

I returned my attention to the presentation I had been working on. Whatever was or wasn't happening between me and Jamison would figure itself out.

For now, I needed to work on saving my business.

Chapter 23

Jamison

Seated in my office, I scrolled through the reports on my screen summarizing the financial position of Freedom Capital Real Estate. They weren't a client, but through my contacts, I was able to pull together non-confidential information.

Tallulah hadn't asked me to do this. In fact, I hadn't heard from her, though I'd told her to let me know how the meeting went. I didn't want to appear desperate, so I hadn't reached out, but I was seriously reconsidering. All I could think about was the way she'd looked up at me when I was in her store last. The slight upturn of her mouth haunted my thoughts, and those lovely brown eyes of hers never failed to send chills down my spine.

I had to talk to her again. I had no choice. But before I reached out, I was doing a little research on the company causing her stress.

A knock on my office door pulled me from my thoughts, and I looked up to find my son standing in the doorway with a folder tucked under his arm, a slightly uncertain expression on his face. I sensed he wasn't completely comfortable coming to me with work-related questions and struggled with having his father as a colleague, though I wasn't his direct supervisor.

"Hey Dad, got a minute?" he asked.

"Always, for you."

I closed the tabs on the screen and gave him my undivided attention as he approached.

He set down the folder and opened it to a credit analysis he had been working on. "I'm having a hard time with this debt ratio calculation. It's an agricultural company, so their revenue stream is irregular because of seasonal variations. I'm not sure if I should use data from the last 12 months or an average of the last three years to account for the irregularities."

I pulled the folder closer and scanned the figures. "It's an agricultural company, so you *have* to account for the seasonality, but you also want to make sure you capture any trending data." I picked up a pen from my desk and made notes in the margin. "I suggest you run the numbers both ways and compare both results. If there's a significant difference, you'll have a good idea about the stability of the operation."

He nodded slowly, leaning over the desk and pulling out his own pen to write a few notes. "I see what you're saying. Show the range of possibilities instead of trying to force a conclusion from one set of numbers."

"Correct. In a case like this, a single data point could lead you to make the wrong decision. You want the full picture, which will be in the best interest of the client and help you make the best decision to assist them."

"Makes sense. Thanks, Dad." He picked up the folder. "You want to grab dinner tonight? Blossom is busy, so you and I could hang out. There's a new Thai place up the street from where I live. We could try it out."

Any other day, any other week, I would've jumped at the

chance to have dinner with my son. Manuel and I didn't spend as much time together as I'd like, and most of the time when I saw him, we were at work. I wanted to maintain a relationship with him as much as possible, even though he was an adult, but I had already made up my mind about my plans for the evening.

"I'll have to take a raincheck," I said. "I have a class."

His eyebrows rose higher. "What class do you have on Monday night?"

"Yoga."

"Yoga?" he said, with a laugh. "When did you start taking yoga?"

"Why are you acting so surprised?"

"Because I've never once in my entire twenty-two years heard you say a word about yoga. Doesn't fit you."

"You don't know what fits me. Besides, I'm almost fifty years old, and I can't lift weights and run around the track forever. People my age need to work on our flexibility, and from my research, yoga is a good exercise to incorporate into my lifestyle."

"*Yoga?*" He stared at me in disbelief.

"Yes, Manuel. Yoga."

"Where are you taking the class?"

I shifted in my chair. "At Ms. Washington's wellness center. They have a Monday night class. She mentioned it once, so I'm going to check it out."

I hadn't told Tallulah I was coming, but I'd already checked online and saw that interested students were encouraged to drop in for a free first class to see if it was a good fit.

"Okay," Manuel murmured, sounding confused. "Enjoy your yoga class, and I guess we'll do dinner another night." He paused on the way to the door. "Do you even have yoga pants?"

"I have athletic wear. That's good enough."

"Okay," he murmured again, still sounding confused.

After he left, I checked my watch. I had enough time to finish up here, go home to change clothes, and then head over to Simply Well. Based on afternoon traffic, I should arrive approximately ten minutes before class started.

Despite not wanting to seem desperate, I was committing an act of desperation. I wanted to see Tallulah. I wanted to be in the same room with her, even if we were only stretching and breathing or whatever they do in yoga classes.

I finished my work and left on time. I went home, changed into a T-shirt and a pair of joggers and tennis shoes, then hopped back into my Lexus and drove over to the plaza. I felt a little ridiculous but also excited and energized.

A sign on the front door instructed me to go around the side. I entered and went down the hall, my heart rate elevated in anticipation of seeing Tallulah. I found the studio easily, a room with wood floors, dark walls—one of them mirrored—and softly playing music. Inside, women of all shapes and sizes talked in quiet tones or stretched in preparation for the class. I immediately spotted the back of Tallulah's head and was relieved she hadn't decided to miss tonight's session. She wore a white tank and green yoga pants that looked fantastic on her ass. No jewelry this time. Her waist-length locs were in a low ponytail and swept over one shoulder. She bent over to roll out her yoga mat like the other women in the room.

Yoga mat!

I hadn't executed my plan as perfectly as I initially thought. I had completely forgotten a very important piece.

A young woman stepped into my line of sight, blocking my view of Tallulah bending over. She looked to be in her twenties and wore a welcoming smile, blue streaks in her brown hair, and multiple earrings climbing up the shell of her right ear.

"Hello, I'm Julie. Welcome to Simply Well yoga. First time?"

"Yes, first time here and first time taking yoga. I wanted to try the class, but..." I dropped my voice. "I forgot to bring a yoga mat."

"Not a problem. I have a couple of extra ones right there," she said, pointing to a corner in the back. "Pick one and find a spot to set up. What's your name?"

"Jamison."

"Nice to meet you, Jamison." She left me to walk toward the front of the room.

I picked up one of the mats as a man walked in. He nodded at me, and I nodded back before seeking out an empty spot. I decided to roll out the mat near the wall to my right.

Tallulah was now sitting cross-legged on the floor, back straight, with her eyes closed and hands resting on her knees. She looked peaceful. Centered. Completely in her element. I almost felt like an intruder and considered backing out, then I changed my mind. I had come this far and wasn't going to leave without talking to her.

I rolled out my mat and attempted to sit cross-legged like she and some of the other women, but my knees immediately protested. Holy shit. What had I gotten myself into? This might be harder than I had anticipated.

More people trickled in over the next few minutes, including one more man. Finally, the music stopped, and Julie sat on her mat in front of the class, also cross-legged.

"Good evening, everyone." She spoke in a hushed voice, hands clasped together in a prayerful pose.

"Good evening," the class returned.

"Namaste," she said with a gentle bow. "Welcome to Monday night yoga at Simply Well. I'm so glad you're all here. This is a no-judgment zone, so don't push yourself beyond..."

I stopped listening, my gaze shifting to Tallulah. She casually scanned the room and did a double take when she saw me.

Her mouth opened slightly, and I watched her expression shift from surprise to confusion to what could only be described as pleasure. I gave her a small nod, and she slowly smiled, nodding back.

Just like that, my uncertainty about coming disappeared. Tallulah Washington smiled at me.

I had made the right decision.

Now I was going to attempt an activity I had never done before. Yoga. Because I couldn't stay away from her.

"We're going to start with child's pose tonight," Julie was saying.

I had no idea what that was, but I watched as she changed position to sit back on her heels and folded forward, resting her head on the floor, arms outstretched.

I followed suit, listening to Julie's soothing voice as she encouraged us to relax and instructed us on how to breathe.

I slowed down mentally, and my muscles loosened as I relaxed into the pose.

This wasn't so bad.

I could handle an hour of yoga.

Chapter 24

Jamison

I had made a terrible mistake and realized too late. Forty minutes into my first and likely last yoga class, I was bent forward trying to touch my toes without looking like a complete idiot.

Spoiler alert: I was failing badly.

"Great job, class," Julie said from the front of the studio. "Hold the position."

She was demonstrating a pose called uttanasana... ucana-bana... something or other. Whatever the name, it was a standing forward bend, and she did it with the ease of someone whose spine and joints were made of jelly.

"Let your head hang heavy, relax your neck, and breathe into the stretch," she continued in her soothing voice.

Breathe into the stretch. Right.

With my head dangling upside down, I looked around the room and was impressed by the form of the other students. Tallulah was folded in half, the ends of her ponytail brushing her yoga mat. I couldn't see her face, but she seemed comfortable and completely at home in her body. Most of the others wore serene expressions with their hands flat on the floor, an impressive feat. The woman to my left had gone into an advanced version of the pose by wrapping her arms between and behind her legs. Meanwhile, I could barely get the tips of my fingers to touch the mat.

My competitive spirit kicked in.

I went to the gym regularly. I was physically fit and not on any prescription medication. I refused to allow a simple forward bend to defeat me.

I sucked in my belly and moved deeper into the stretch. My hamstrings protested the unfamiliar position, but I ignored the warning. Each week I ran five miles on the treadmill. I had played soccer on a rec team in college. No way was a simple forward bend going to break me.

"Remember," Julie said, walking between the mats. "Don't compare yourself to anyone else."

Too late.

"Stay in your comfort zone and breathe."

I wasn't sure where my comfort zone was located, and breathing proved difficult as I tried not to grunt like a bear lifting weights in the forest.

I challenged myself to go deeper, and that's when a sharp, painful tug lanced through my left hamstring.

"Ah!" The sound escaped before I could stop it. Part gasp, part cry. Definitely a sound that didn't belong in the calm tranquility of a yoga studio.

Heads turned in my direction.

I jerked upright, immediately regretting the move as pain cut through the muscles in the back of my thigh.

"Are you okay?" Julie appeared at my side with amazing quickness, probably no stranger to dealing with overzealous beginners.

"Fine," I said in a pained voice. "I might have stretched a little too far."

"You should probably sit down." Her voice was kind but firm.

Tallulah watched me with concern in her eyes, and I saw the exact moment she understood what had happened. She rushed over to me.

"What did you hurt?" she asked.

"Hamstring. Left side." I tried to lower myself gracefully to the mat but failed, dropping to the floor with the elegance of a felled tree.

"Try extending your leg," Julie suggested.

I did as she asked, but another sharp pain lanced through my thigh, and I winced in agony, gritting my teeth to keep from crying out again. "Not a good idea," I said.

"We need to put ice on the muscle. I'll help you up, and then you can lean on me to walk, okay?" Tallulah said.

"I can walk," I insisted, though I wasn't one hundred percent certain. All I knew was I'd crawl out of there on my hands and knees before I leaned my weight on her.

Both she and Julie helped me to my feet.

"Lean on me," Tallulah said, positioning herself under my arm.

"No."

"Jamison—"

"*I'm fine*," I insisted.

Some of the students were sneaking glances at us.

"Let me help," she hissed.

"Go. I'll follow."

We had a staring contest.

"I'm so sorry this happened," Julie said.

I had forgotten she was standing nearby.

"I'm sorry for disrupting your class."

She shot me a sympathetic smile. "These things can happen when you push too far. As Tallulah said, ice the muscle and take some ibuprofen. Next time, don't force the stretch."

She actually thought there would be a next time. Cute.

I followed Tallulah out of the room, limping the entire way but determined not to put my weight on her. Our progress toward the front of the center was slow but not entirely bad. I had the pleasure of watching her firm bottom as she walked ahead of me. The color green never looked so good.

Tallulah led me into her small office behind the counter, a room the size of a closet, with a desk and two chairs crammed inside. Different colored sticky notes littered the wall above the desk with reminders and affirmations scribbled on them in her terrible handwriting. Without a word, she pointed at the chair closest to me, her stony silence a clear indication she was upset with me for not accepting her help.

I grunted as I dropped into the chair.

She disappeared and then returned a few minutes later with a bottle of water and a bag of frozen peas wrapped in a thin cloth.

"Where did you get the peas?" I asked.

She knelt beside the chair. "The Asian market next door. Lift your leg as much as you can."

I did and groaned at the painful pull of my muscles. She placed the peas under my thigh. The cold was shocking but also provided relief.

"Keep the bag there for twenty minutes."

"Thank you."

"I hope you didn't do serious damage."

She leaned against the desk. In the small space, I was inches away from her. My eyes traveled over the curve of her hips and the fullness of her breasts in the tight tank, then traveled higher to the ropelike hairs hanging over her shoulder. I itched to touch them again, winding them around my hand as I had during the time she spent in my bed.

She crossed her arms. "Was this your first yoga class?"

"Actually, no. It was my last yoga class."

She fought a smile and lost, the corners of her mouth tilting upward slightly. "Why were you in the class in the first place?"

I shifted in the chair to buy time. What should I say? "I was curious about yoga and figured it might be something I could incorporate into my schedule—assuming I liked it."

"Oh really?" She obviously didn't believe me. "Why did you pick *this* particular class? They teach yoga at the brand new, state-of-the-art gym where you have a membership."

"Do they?"

She narrowed her eyes. "I'm sure you know they do."

I met her gaze. "You're right, they have yoga. But they don't have you."

My bold statement changed the air, and I was immediately reminded of us dancing in my living room, of kissing her soft lips, of holding her in my arms, and the breathy sounds she made as I thrust into her.

"Are you trying to sweet talk me?"

"Maybe." I screwed the top off the bottle of water and took a swig. "I have a second reason for coming here. You didn't tell me how the presentation to Mr. Ochoa went."

Her expression clouded. "Do you want the bad news or the bad news?"

Oh no. "What happened?"

She sighed, perching on the edge of the desk. "We presented our case, which included listing the length of time long-term tenants had been there. We talked about the sense of community and shared testimonials from our customers."

"Let me guess, Ochoa didn't care."

"He listened and then said he appreciated our efforts, but

sob stories don't pay the bills." For the first time since I'd known her, bitterness crept into Tallulah's voice. "I asked him to give us one more shot to convince him, and he agreed we could return on Friday with a more convincing presentation, or the rent increases would go through. We have no idea what to tell him to make our case, but we're working on collecting those extra signatures I told you about."

I adjusted the peas under my leg. "Did your presentation include showing him how costly turnover would be?"

"You told me to include that type of information, and I discussed it with the team, but we didn't know how to convey that message to him." She seemed agitated.

"Emotion doesn't work on people like Ochoa," I said carefully. "They care about their bottom line, which is basically what he told you. But after being in banking for years, I will say most landlords don't consider the expense of tenant turnover."

"How expensive is it?"

"Depends, but they risk losing between six months to a year of rent. They might also have to pay improvement costs for the new occupant, along with broker fees and, in some cases, legal costs. If the new tenant doesn't work out and can't pay the rent, they have another set of problems."

"How do we prove what you said? Is there a report I can take to him? A study?"

An outline of the argument formed in my head. "You need to pull together vacancy rates in the area and other figures to show his potential revenue loss compared to the guaranteed income from retaining stable, long-term tenants."

"How do I do that?" she sounded exasperated.

"You don't have to. I will."

Tallulah looked at me with brief surprise. "I wasn't asking you to—"

"I know. I'm offering."

"You don't have to," Tallulah said quietly.

"I want to."

Those three words seemed to lift a weight off her shoulders.

"You have until Friday, which is only four days away, but I can pull together a solid presentation in a short amount of time. I'm meeting clients for dinner tomorrow night, but I'm free Wednesday night. We could work on the revised presentation then."

Appreciation shone in her eyes. "Why are you doing this?" she asked softly.

Because you're constantly on my mind. Because helping you feels like the right thing to do. Because I want you to turn to me when life gets hard.

None of those words left my mouth. Instead, I said, "I'm good at this kind of thing. Let me help."

Pursing her lips, she still appeared hesitant. "Okay, Wednesday. Where?"

"We can work at my place, in my home office."

"Your place." She said the words as if she remembered, like I did, all the ways we had driven each other wild the last time she stepped foot in my home. "Sounds good."

We tossed around a few ideas for the presentation, and then I checked my watch. More than twenty minutes had passed. I removed the cold bag and cautiously straightened my leg. The muscle still hurt, but less than before.

"Better?" Tallulah asked, eyeing my thigh.

"Yes."

"Ice it again when you get home, and take an ibuprofen."

"Yes, ma'am."

She rolled her eyes. "I'm serious. Be careful or you'll be limping for weeks."

Standing slowly, I tested my weight on the leg. Tallulah

pushed away from the desk and reached to help, but I waved her off.

"I'm good."

"Are you sure?"

"Positive. The pain isn't as bad as before."

I had taken the side entrance to come into the class, but my car was parked out front, so she let me out the front door. I paused on my way out and reached for her, stroking her arm and enjoying the softness of her skin.

"Thank you."

"You're welcome."

"FYI, I won't be back."

She laughed. "I know."

We gazed at each other, and then I inhaled the inviting scent of her vanilla and honey body cream—the same scent that had lingered in my sheets after she left my bed.

"I'll see you Wednesday. Come by after you close the store. I'll order dinner for us."

She looked up at me with her inviting brown eyes, her lips slightly parted. I leaned down and kissed her. I couldn't help myself.

She sighed softly as I withdrew.

"Wednesday," I said again.

"Wednesday," she whispered.

I stepped out into the cool night air and limped to my car. There was no graceful way to walk away from her, each painful step a reminder of how my ego had overridden common sense.

As I slid behind the wheel, I saw her standing in the doorway in her white tank, green skin-tight yoga pants, and her hair thrown over one shoulder.

Yes, I had suffered a minor injury tonight.

But it was worth it.

Chapter 25

Tallulah

I arrived at Jamison's condo in the early evening, nerves fluttering in my stomach. The last time I was there, we had scorched the sheets and the chair in his bedroom, and my internal temperature rose at the memories as I stood outside.

When he opened the door, I inhaled silently, memories of our lovemaking flooding back. Then, of course, there was the kiss he had given me at the center before limping away. Barely a moment had passed when I hadn't relived his lips on mine.

"Come in," Jamison said.

I stepped across the threshold, and he led me into the kitchen.

"I ordered sushi, and then thought... what if she doesn't eat sushi? If you don't, I can order something different for your dinner."

He was so considerate. "I love sushi," I assured him, placing my cloth bag with my computer and notes on the counter.

Jamison's small galley kitchen opened on both ends, so it didn't seem cramped. On the other side was a dining area with a polished mahogany table and four chairs. The rest of his home was exactly as I remembered—very neat and orderly, and I was certain he hadn't straightened up because I was coming over. This was the norm.

The decor consisted of clean lines and neutral colors everywhere. A charcoal sectional faced a mounted flat-screen TV, and against one wall were built-in shelves holding mostly nonfiction books.

"How is your leg?" I asked.

"Much better," he replied, sounding relieved. He removed two plates from a cabinet. "I haven't gone to the gym or done any strenuous activities. Taking it easy is my motto for now."

He handed me a plate, and I selected pieces from the containers of food he had set out. Afterward, he poured himself a glass of wine, but I opted for water, and we ate at the small table.

We started off talking about the kids and the wedding, and I slipped in one or two teasing remarks about his venture into yoga, but most of our conversation centered around the plans for the building.

After dinner, Jamison led me down the hallway. When we passed the door leading to his bedroom, I purposely kept my eyes straight ahead, focused on his back.

His home office was impressive. A large cherrywood desk facing the window contained two monitors. An expensive-looking laser printer sat atop a three-drawer file cabinet made of the same cherrywood. Unsurprisingly, his desk was organized with the same precision as the rest of his home. Pens were in a holder, papers were neatly arranged in clear organizers, and not a sticky note in sight. His skin must have been crawling in my tiny office.

He sat behind the desk and pulled another chair around next to it. "Ready to work?"

"As ready as I'll ever be."

We worked for at least an hour, revising the PowerPoint presentation to include not only my original tenant surveys and community impact stories but also Jamison's financial projections and market analysis. I was impressed by the thoroughness of his research.

He pointed a pen at one of the monitors. "What do you think about this slide? I'm thinking we should mention specific numbers. For instance, your notes say Leslie's coffee shop is a daily stop for the office workers on the upper floors, and the print shop handles a few of the corporate accounts. We need the exact numbers and should include others, like the Far East Market. How many people come in there after work to purchase items before going home? We could also mention the bakery if Shelley has hard numbers to provide, and then transition to the financial stability argument."

Studying the slide, I was impressed by how he had woven hard data with the human element. "I like your idea. It suggests we're not just small businesses, we're also part of the building's ecosystem."

"It's not a suggestion. You *are* a part of the ecosystem," he said in a firm voice. "The plaza works because of the relationships established among the tenants on the first two floors and the professional offices above. Ochoa runs the risk of disrupting this synergy by bringing in new tenants who might not integrate well."

I nodded. "Sounds logical. Obvious."

He moved to the next slide. "Ochoa is looking at raw numbers and not considering intangible value—things like the stability of the businesses already there and how each one helps to make the building attractive to the people upstairs, as well as casual passersby."

His fingers moved quickly over the keyboard, his brow

furrowed in concentration. He was in his element, problem-solving and analyzing to find a solution.

And he was doing it for me.

"Jamison." I said his name in a low voice.

He looked up, his eyes questioning.

I opened my mouth to express my appreciation and tell him how much his efforts meant to me, but I surprised myself by saying something entirely different. "What if this doesn't work?" I had voiced my fears out loud.

"The presentation? We can revise—"

"No, I mean... what if we do everything right and put together a stellar presentation, and Mr. Ochoa doesn't care? What if he doesn't care about community value and ecosystem synergy? What if he doesn't care about the numbers and just wants us out so he can make more money the way he believes is best?"

Jamison twisted the chair to face me fully. "I'm confident we're putting together a stronger presentation, but if it doesn't work, you can find a new location."

I shook my head. "A new place won't be the same. The building has a new name, which was jarring enough, but the location is perfect. It's where I built my business from scratch."

"Tallulah, you can build again somewhere else."

He didn't understand, and I felt the familiar tightness that appeared in my chest whenever I considered the possibility of losing Simply Well. "You make starting over sound so easy."

His face turned sympathetic. "It's not easy, but it can be done."

"Can it?" The words came out with more bitterness than I intended. "Maybe this is proof I was never supposed to have a business in the first place. My ex-husband used to say I was too flighty and idealistic. He said I didn't understand how the real world worked, and now I'm wondering if he was right. I put so much into Simply Well all these years, and now a buyout could wipe out all my hard work."

Jamison's expression hardened. "He wasn't right."

"You don't know that."

"Yes, I do. You've been running a successful business for ten years, in a very precarious industry, I might add. You beat the odds by staying open. For ten years, you've helped people, built a client base, and become a meaningful part of the community. Far from flighty, your work is real and powerful."

"But if I lose it all—"

"A setback doesn't wipe out a decade of success." He moved closer, his eyes intense. "I'm sure you've faced challenges before in this business. The change coming from the new landlord is another one, a big one, but you're not facing the situation alone. You have the other tenants behind you. You're also not unprepared. The tenants are organized, you gathered information from them, and you're putting together a strategic response through a presentation. You're not flighty, Tallulah. You're a smart businesswoman, and if by chance this doesn't work—which I'm fairly confident it will—I know you can start over and be successful again."

I desperately wanted to believe him. "When I told you that I tended to go with the flow, I wasn't exaggerating," I said quietly. "Other than my beautiful daughter, this business is my greatest accomplishment. I hate to think I might lose it because I didn't plan better, because I didn't prepare for a raise in the rent or—"

"Stop." Jamison gripped my hands in his. "No one could have predicted this. My specialty is commercial banking, and having a business can be extremely volatile with changes all the time. Landlords shift their priorities for any number of reasons. What's happening has nothing to do with a failure to plan. It simply was outside anyone's control."

"But I don't have a backup plan because I just go with the flow," I said, my voice shaky.

His expression softened. "We need more people like you in the world, believe me. Without you, the rest of us wouldn't have any fun, and life would be boring as hell."

Despite my worries, I smiled. "Boring is safe."

"Safe is overrated."

"You don't believe that for a second. If I had to guess, safe is your middle name. You probably have a five-year financial plan mapped out."

He released me.

"I have a ten-year plan, but that's not the point." He looked deeply into my eyes. "Your approach to life, where you depend on intuition and creativity and you're willing to take risks based on your own beliefs—that's valuable, Tallulah. That's how you built Simply Well into the place it is today."

My throat tightened with emotion.

"You do not want to be more like me," he said dryly. "I've spent my entire adult life playing it safe, coloring within the lines, planning, and using structure to guide my every step. All to minimize risk. What do I have to show for it? Sure, I have a successful career, but maybe if I had taken more risks, I could be farther along, in a higher position. My marriage failed, and my son forced me to take dance lessons because I'm so stiff and rigid."

I touched his knee. "You're being too hard on yourself."

"And so are you." His hand covered mine, threading his fingers between my fingers. "I know we're different, but being different doesn't mean one of us is right and the other is wrong. We can balance each other out."

"Is that what we're doing? Balancing each other?" I held my breath as I waited for his answer, fully aware I was asking about more than the work on the computer.

"I believe so. If you'll let me," he replied quietly.

I examined our intertwined fingers—his large and pale, mine smaller, dark, and decorated with rings. We were different in so many ways, yet we fit together.

He squeezed my fingers and lifted the back of my hand to his lips. "You're going to be fine. I'm going to do everything I can to make sure of it, starting with this excellent PowerPoint presentation." He smiled.

I smiled back. "If Ochoa doesn't like it, I'll be fine," I said, my confidence slowly returning.

"Exactly. Now, I have another idea..."

We spent the next thirty minutes discussing lease terms and current turnover costs and all kinds of things I had never considered or heard about.

I valued Jamison's suggestions.

I trusted him.

Not only with this business presentation but with my heart. Going with the flow had seen me through some tough periods in my life, but I was starting to see the value in stopping, thinking, and using a measured approach.

Jamison made me realize I was hanging onto some of the negative comments my ex-husband had made in the past. His assessment had lingered in the back of my mind, but Jamison's comments helped me see my strengths were as valuable as anyone else's.

I sat back in the chair, enjoying the simple pleasure of watching him work. He was loving this, and I loved this feeling of being part of a team for the first time in a long time. This feeling of not having to figure out everything alone.

Maybe a rigid tightwad wasn't so bad after all. As long as his name was Jamison Harris.

Chapter 26

Jamison

Too flighty. Too idealistic.

I couldn't believe Tallulah's ex-husband actually said those words to her. What an idiot.

Pissed me off watching her doubt herself because of him. She was confident in other areas of her life: running the center, sharing her herbal knowledge to help clients—and non-clients like me—and raising her daughter. Yet the possibility of losing Simply Well had caused her confidence to crumble, making me want to find her ex and have a man-to-man talk about the lasting damage of his careless words.

More than ever, I wanted to make damn sure she won over Ochoa.

I glanced at the spreadsheet on the second monitor. "I think we're done here. We covered the benefits of long-term leases, stable tenants, et cetera..." My voice faded as I clicked a tab to look at other numbers. "We've done a good job of showing the financial benefits Freedom Capital Real Estate gains from keeping the current roster of tenants."

Tallulah pulled her chair closer to see the spreadsheet better, and I caught a whiff of her.

I focused on the numbers instead of her closeness. "When you talk to him, spend time on this slide, drilling home the point that when a tenant leaves, they don't only lose rent during a vacancy period. Potentially, this is what it could cost them."

Her eyebrows lifted in surprise.

"Sometimes more, depending on the space and the market," I added.

Tallulah was quiet for a moment. "I understand what the landlord has to lose, but what if we offered an incentive to keep us? Something extra to make the whole plaza more valuable."

I sat back. "I'm listening."

Excitement bloomed in her pretty eyes as the idea took shape. "The first two floors are all small businesses, most owner-operated. The upper floors are professional offices with accountants, lawyers, a marketing firm, and so on. Some of these people are already customers, but most aren't. What if we could market to more of them through a partnership program? For instance, Sugar Crumb Bakery could offer catering discounts. I could offer corporate wellness classes on stress management, and Julie could do a yoga-at-lunch kind of thing. The print shop already does quite a bit of work for those businesses, but I'm sure Tyler wouldn't mind formalizing a discount structure if it helped bring in more business. Do you see where I'm going with this?"

"Brilliant."

Her face brightened. "Yeah?"

"Absolutely. The partnership you're suggesting would integrate the business community even more, and Ochoa could use it as a selling point to attract new professional tenants upstairs." My mind was already racing with the implications. "He could market the plaza as not only office space but a self-contained location with additional built-in amenities."

A broad grin spread across her face.

"Your idea will allow him to differentiate his property from other plazas in the area. This could be huge." I created another slide. "Tenants will get office space and access to a network of service providers."

"I hadn't thought about the partnership exactly that way, but I like the way you said it."

"You were thinking about community and mutual support, which is fine. I'm simply translating your idea into language Ochoa will understand and appreciate. By offering the professionals discounts and special deals through your businesses, he'll have a competitive advantage and could optimize revenue."

"Love it. Yes!" I wanted to jump up and scream with joy but refrained.

We spent the next hour building out the partnership program concept and refining the presentation to show how its incorporation would positively affect Ochoa's bottom line.

When we finished, I strongly believed the new proposal was a better, more proactive plan than the first. I saved the files and backed them up in three different locations. Then I turned to Tallulah. "Ochoa would be a fool not to accept this idea."

"Let's hope he's not a fool, shall we?"

We both laughed. I was pleased to see the joy and relief on her face.

"I can't thank you enough for helping me—us. And for believing in me."

"I know we haven't known each other long, but you're an amazing woman. You care about people. You're kind. You work hard. You're remarkable."

"You're going to make me blush," she said.

I took her hand in mine. "I meant every word."

"You're pretty amazing yourself. I had no idea what we were going to do, but you stepped in and reorganized our argument and used all the right words."

"We make a good team."

"We do," she agreed.

The air between us shifted, becoming charged with awareness. She was a stunning woman, tonight wearing a dress in a riot of color—deep reds, electric blues, and splashes of turquoise and gold. Against the canvas of her chestnut-brown skin, the outfit was like a work of art. The deep neckline gathered beneath her chest and turned into generous folds of soft material, while the three-quarter-length sleeves hung below her elbows in a dramatic fashion.

"We should celebrate," I said, my voice dropping lower.

"How?"

"With a kiss." I pulled her onto my lap, and with a soft laugh, she rested her hands on my shoulders.

"This seems self-serving," she whispered.

"Guilty as charged."

Her eyes darkened, and I leaned in to kiss her.

I tasted her lips, flicking my tongue at the corner of her mouth. "I can't stop thinking about you. Us. How good we are together."

"We are good together, aren't we?"

"Surprisingly good," I whispered.

We kissed again, and I cupped Tallulah's jaw, tempering the heat and slowing us down. I didn't want explosive and hot like the first time. I wanted slow and deliberate so I could savor every moment she remained in my arms.

I took my time relearning her mouth, listening to her satisfied sighs, arms around my neck, her breasts pressed against my chest. I caressed her buttocks and thighs, groaning softly as I enjoyed her womanly shape. I'd missed this. Not only the physical contact but the emotional intimacy.

My body hardened as renewed need charged through me.

"Bedroom?" I murmured huskily against her mouth.

"Yes."

We made our way to my bedroom without the urgent, frantic need of the last time. I lowered the dress off one shoulder and kissed her bared skin, going lower to the swell of her breast and inhaling her intoxicating scent.

I unwrapped her like a present, taking my time to kiss each newly exposed inch of dark skin. She did the same, her hands gently removing my clothes, her eyes filled with tenderness as she gazed up at me and offered her mouth again.

When our bodies finally joined on top of my bed, it was quieter than the explosive passion of the first time.

"God, you're beautiful... incredible," I whispered into her collarbone.

My hips worked between her spread thighs, one hand cupping her bottom to bring her tighter against me, allowing me to go deeper. She was slick and warm and felt like heaven.

I watched her face and her passion-glazed eyes, learning exactly which movements made her breath catch and which made her face crumble with pleasure.

"You're perfect," she whispered, slipping her fingers into my hair.

We moved together in sync, with the same rhythm we had found on the dance floor. She followed my lead, her hips quickening or slowing at my direction. No thinking about what came next, no planning the future, just this moment and this connection and the building pressure that wound tighter with every thrust.

Finally, her hands gripped my shoulders, and my name fell

from her lips in fragmented syllables. Her feminine muscles tightened around me, and my own control began to slip.

I kissed her as we climbed the peak together.

"Jamison," she gasped. "I'm—"

"Yeah. Me too."

I captured her mouth with a surge of brutal passion, my thrusts faster and deeper as we tumbled together into ecstasy. Pleasure crashed through me as her body trembled beneath mine. The intensity and intimacy of coming at the same time stole my breath.

I groaned and pressed my face into the side of her neck, straining my hard body into her softer one before collapsing, spent, beside her.

My heart hammered in my chest as I stared up at the dark ceiling. I pulled her into my arms and kissed her forehead. Her hair had fallen out of her updo and lay strewn across the pillow.

"That was..." she started.

"Yeah."

There was nothing more to say. The emotions coursing through me were more than mere attraction. More than chemistry. I risked falling for Tallulah.

She pressed a kiss to my chest, and I squeezed her closer. I wanted her beside me every single day, which meant I was in serious trouble.

I hadn't just fallen for Tallulah. I had already fallen.

And for once in my carefully planned life, I wasn't afraid of where I might land.

* * *

"You had to pick tea," I said.

We were sitting up in my bed, naked and under the covers,

talking. She had an arm and a leg thrown across me, her head resting on my shoulder.

"How was I supposed to know you hate tea?" she asked. "Who despises tea that much? It's a very specific thing to hate. What's your problem?"

"I don't have a problem," I denied.

"You definitely have a problem," she insisted.

I sighed. "There might be a story behind my distaste for tea."

"I knew it!" She lifted onto her elbow to see my face. "Go on."

I chuckled softly, feeling ridiculous for having to explain the origin of my hang-up. "Goes back to my childhood. My parents used to make iced tea a lot, usually unsweetened unless they were splurging and used sugar. Remember I told you we were poor? We used to reuse the bags, which made the drink watered down on top of being sugarless. But we didn't have much choice. You drank watered-down tea or water. When I became an adult, I avoided tea at all costs but discovered coffee in college. I used it to stay awake since I was working full-time while going to school. You could say I developed a bit of an addiction."

"Now I understand. For the record, there are all kinds of teas, and they offer great benefits. I'll bring you one of my blends, and you can tell me what you think."

Typical Tallulah. Thoughtful. Kind. "I appreciate the offer. So you plan to come back? Because I think you should come back as often as possible." I trailed my finger down the middle of her chest to the v-shaped curly hairs cradled between her hips.

"Since you're inviting me, I'll come back for sure, which is better than inviting myself and coming across as desperate."

I arched an eyebrow at her. "Desperate? Let me tell you

about desperate. Desperate is wanting to see a certain wellness center owner and pretending to be interested in yoga so you don't come across as desperate."

"Oh, honey. You could have just called me up and asked me out." She cupped my face. "But I like a little desperation in my men."

Cupping her hand against my cheek, I turned fully sideways to gaze into her eyes. "I'm your man now?"

"If you want to be."

"I very much want to be."

"Then yes. And I'm your woman," she said softly.

"I like how that sounds." I leaned in and kissed her. It should have been short and quick, but she was intoxication personified.

The next thing I knew, my tongue was in her mouth, and I was on top of her, nestled between her thighs, ready for another round.

Chapter 27

Tallulah

I rolled out of bed late Sunday morning after taking a nap to recuperate from my night with Jamison.

We had gone to a nighttime festival, where local artisans showcased their art, music, and food. I left with delicious crusty bread and two jars of jam I was eager to try. Then Jamison and I went dancing, which kept us out late—but not too late. We were Gen-Xers, after all. It was nice to wake up in his arms, cook breakfast together, and enjoy a leisurely meal before coming home.

But I was still tired, and the nap had rejuvenated me.

I stood in the bathroom, brushing my teeth, thinking about how magical the past two weeks had been. Leslie, Tyler, and I met with Ochoa and his team again and presented the revised presentation. Though we had to wait a full two weeks to hear from him, I had suspected we would have good news based on his improved attitude when we met.

Sure enough, last Friday he reached out and confirmed he liked our ideas, and with a few tweaks to the partnership program, he wanted to roll it out right away. He also wanted to lock us all into longer-term leases, which all the owners except one accepted because she planned to sell her business.

Jamison and I talked every night and occasionally during the day, but the weekend belonged to us. My daughter knew I was seeing someone, but she was preoccupied with planning her wedding, which meant Jamison and I could spend time together without me having to explain my behavior to my nosy daughter.

Wrapped in a colorful silk robe and with my hair down around my shoulders, I strolled into the kitchen. Blossom sat at the table, looking at something on her phone, her bare feet tucked under her on the chair.

"Morning," I said in a cheerful voice.

"Morning," she said, lifting her gaze before returning her attention to the phone. "You're in a good mood."

"It's a pretty day. I'm alive. I can't complain. Have you eaten already?"

"Yes. I ate at Manuel's before I came home."

"How is my future son-in-law? Haven't seen him in a while." I opened the refrigerator and removed one of my wellness shots.

"Hmm."

I tossed back the drink. As usual, the ginger burned a little as it went down. "What does hmm mean?"

"We went over the wedding budget by a few thousand dollars, and he's being a pain."

"Do you need help?" I asked.

"No, no, it's fine. We'll figure it out."

"Are you sure?"

"I'm sure, I promise. Forget I mentioned it." She waved her hand dismissively. "Did you hear from the landlord yet?"

"Oh, I haven't had a chance to tell you because we haven't seen each other. They accepted our proposal!"

"That's fantastic!"

"I know. I can't believe it." I then explained what would happen next.

"You took the lead, didn't you? So your ideas won them over."

"Well, they weren't only my ideas," I hedged. I poured myself a glass of orange juice.

"I know Leslie and Mr. Morris helped, but you did a lot of work on the project. You should be proud."

"I am proud, but I can't take all the credit, like I said. I had help, other than Leslie and Tyler."

"Who else helped you?"

I hesitated. Jamison and I agreed we needed to tell the kids about our relationship, but we deemed it best to wait until after the wedding, which was only two weeks away.

"Manuel's father. Jamison." I drank the juice and then placed the glass on the counter.

"Oh."

That one word carried a lot of weight. Neither of us spoke for a while.

"It's great that you're getting along so well," Blossom said. "Interestingly enough, Manuel said his father took yoga a while back, and he had never done that before or shown any interest in yoga."

Why was Manuel always sharing his father's business?

"People change as they get older, develop new interests and drop others." I moved around the kitchen on autopilot, rinsing a mug I hadn't even used and setting it on the drying rack.

"Just seemed strange since he passed on spending time with Manuel to go to the class."

"Did he?" I tried to sound neutral, but my voice became higher at the end, and I could feel Blossom's bold stare in the back of my head.

"You know what I was thinking the other day," she continued. "You haven't dated anyone seriously since you and Dad divorced."

This was not the conversation I expected to have on Sunday morning. I turned to face her. "I have dated," I said carefully.

"Not seriously."

Crossing my arms, I leaned my hip against the counter. "What made you think about my dating history?"

My daughter shrugged. "I don't know. I guess because our lives are changing. Manuel and I are getting married in a couple of weeks, and I'll be moving out permanently. And you've been... different."

"Different how?"

As far as I knew, I was behaving the same. Wasn't I?

"I can't quite put my finger on what's changed. You seem more settled or maybe more content?" She placed the phone on the table. "You've been alone a long time, Mom."

Her words landed hard, a glaring indictment of my life since the divorce.

"I haven't been lonely," I said.

"I didn't say lonely. I said alone."

The silence stretched between us, thick but not uncomfortable.

"Is it safe to say you're seeing someone now—someone you like a lot?" she asked.

"Yes." I didn't see the point in lying, and if she point-blank asked me about Jamison, I would tell the truth. I wasn't ashamed of our relationship. We had just decided to keep it under wraps a little bit longer.

Blossom inhaled, as if she had made a decision. "You're seeing Mr. Harris, aren't you?"

There it was.

Before I answered the question, I had to know what specifically gave me away. "Why do you think I'm seeing Jamison?"

"Because he helped you with the presentation, and the whole yoga thing was weird. The two of you were super close at the bakery, and I also remember the day I came by the store for food and he was there. I knew something was off, but I was too preoccupied with looking for work to pay close attention. Also, you don't roll your eyes or look annoyed when his name comes up anymore."

I was impressed by her deductive reasoning. "Yes, Jamison and I are seeing each other."

I braced myself, unsure how she would react. I expected at least a gasp, maybe a horrified expression. Possibly a *"Mom, he's my future father-in-law."* None of that happened.

She nodded slowly, as if everything made sense now. "I figured."

I pushed away from the counter and sat at the table across from her. "We didn't plan to get involved, and I know it's complicated, and whatever you feel—"

"Mom," she said, gently interrupting, "I'm not upset. I think it's great. Now I don't have to worry about you."

I sat up straight. "What do you mean?"

"Like I said, I'll be moving in with Manuel pretty soon. When I was in college, I came home on weekends and holidays, but now you'll be all alone—permanently. I know you'll be fine, but even if you weren't, you would pretend you were. I didn't want that for you."

My throat tightened.

"I love Dad, but I know he wasn't always nice to you. I heard the comments he made, and I figured that's why you've been careful since the divorce."

Was that what I had been? Careful? I hadn't sat down and really examined how I had been living since my divorce from

Karl. But if I had to define my romantic life post-marriage, careful was a fair assessment.

Blossom reached for my hand and squeezed. "Look, I don't need details because... ew, but I like the idea of you and Mr. Harris together. You'll be good for each other. You'll loosen him up, and he'll keep you grounded."

Emotion swelled in my chest, and I patted my thigh. "Come here."

Blossom stood and sat on my lap. This might well be the last time she ever did.

She wrapped her arms around me, and I hugged her, breathing in her unique scent and remembering when she used to fit under my chin instead of looking down at me like she did as an adult.

"Satisfy my curiosity. The night you came in late and locked the door, had you been with Mr. Harris then too?"

"Yes. It was our first time... *together*."

She gasped. "So you've been keeping your relationship a secret all this time?"

"It wasn't really a relationship then, but I would say we have been keeping it a secret the past couple of weeks as we've been trying to make a go of it."

"Do you love him?"

"We care about each other," I said.

I shied away from using the word love at the moment. I don't know why. If anything, my daughter had shown me there was no timeframe around falling in love. Not when you met your person. But I think much of my hesitation came from fear. I wasn't quite ready to say I loved Jamison yet.

"Good enough. You deserve someone who makes you happy, and you deserve a life outside of being my mom."

I shook my head in disbelief. "Such wise words. I guess I didn't do too badly raising you. You had me worried for a while, though, when you accepted a piece of paper as an engagement ring."

She grinned. "Come on. You know it was symbolic."

I grunted. "Symbolic of lack of preparation."

She rolled her eyes. "Doesn't matter now, does it? I have a ring." She held up her hand so I could see. "And I'm getting married in two weeks."

"Yay!"

"Yay!" Blossom threw up her hands in joyous abandonment.

I couldn't be happier for her.

Chapter 28

Tallulah

"I like edgy comedy, but the second guy was too much," Jamison said as we walked up the steps of my front porch. "He wasn't edgy. He was being offensive for the shock value."

We had just returned from dinner and a comedy show. I wore a light sweater over my blouse to guard against the cool night air. "Some of the jokes landed. The bit about his cousins was funny."

"The first part, *maybe*. But then he kept going on and on and crossed the line, in my opinion."

I enjoyed our back-and-forth, disagreeing without being argumentative. Quite a difference from the first time we met.

"What did you think about the opening act? She was hilarious," I said. "When she talked about explaining cryptocurrency to her grandfather, I almost passed out from laughing."

"She was genuinely funny," Jamison conceded, his mouth quirking into the smile I'd come to adore. "When her grandfather scolded her about imaginary money..."

We broke into laughter, the sound floating on the air into the night.

It was after eleven, later than we had planned to stay out, but the show had started late, and after a standing ovation, the third comedian did an encore we didn't want to miss.

Jamison moved closer, his hand finding the small of my back. "Going to the show was a good idea."

"I'm glad you enjoyed yourself, even with the offensive comedian."

"He gave us something to argue about on the drive here."

His head dipped to mine, and I placed my hands on his shoulders, lifting onto my toes to meet him halfway. Our kiss was soft and unhurried, suggesting we had all the time in the world. When he slipped a hand up my spine and into my loose hair, I tightened my arms around his neck and leaned into him.

The headlights of a vehicle swept over us, and we pulled apart, turning our attention to the driveway where a black sedan was rolling to a stop. Blossom climbed out. I immediately smiled, but when she stepped into the porch light, I saw her face, and the smile died on my lips.

Her cheeks were tear-stained, and her eyes were red and swollen.

"Blossom?" I asked sharply, confused and worried by her appearance.

She glanced at me and Jamison, and her face crumpled, fresh tears spilling from her eyes.

"Blossom, what's wrong?" I moved toward her, my heart racing with the horror of knowing my child was hurting. I was ready to do battle with whomever or whatever was making her cry.

But she just shook her head and pushed past us. Fumbling with her keys at the front door, her hands shook so badly that she dropped them on the porch.

I bent to pick them up, but she snatched them before I could and unlocked the door, not once turning her head in my direction. She disappeared inside, leaving me and Jamison standing outside in shocked silence.

"What do you think happened?"

"I don't know, but I'm going to find out." I gently touched his arm. "I'll call you later."

His expression tightened with worry, as if she were his own daughter. "Do you think this is related to Manuel? I'll try to reach him on the way home. Give me an update as soon as you can."

"I will."

He kissed my forehead and squeezed my hand before heading to his vehicle. Inside was quiet, but as I went down the hall, I heard muffled sobbing coming from Blossom's room.

Dread knotted my stomach as I knocked softly on her door. "Blossom? May I come in?"

She didn't answer. I heard continued sobbing, so I didn't know if she heard me.

I opened the door anyway and found her curled on her side, facing the wall with her back to the door, her body shaking from the force of her tears. The sight of her like this—my engaging, funny daughter reduced to raw anguish—made my chest ache.

I crossed the room. Sitting on the edge of the mattress, I placed a hand on her shoulder. "Blossom, my love, what happened?"

Her sobs intensified.

"Talk to me. Please." I rubbed gentle circles on her back, the way I used to when she was little and had nightmares. "Whatever is wrong, we can figure out the solution together."

"There's nothing to figure out." She choked out the words between sobs. "It's over. The wedding is off."

The words crashed into me with the force of a physical blow. "What do you mean the wedding is off?"

What could possibly have happened? They were supposed to get married next week. The rehearsal dinner was planned, friends and family coming to town, and her dress was hanging in the closet.

"Exactly what I said." Her voice was muffled against her pillow. She sniffed. "I can't marry him, Mom. I won't."

"But... why not?" I struggled to process what was happening.

"I don't want to talk about it."

"Blossom—"

"*Please.*" She curled tighter into herself. "I can't. Not right now."

Concerned and feeling completely helpless, I kept my hand on her back. The problem wasn't wedding jitters or cold feet. A deeper issue had emerged and shattered their relationship.

"Did Manuel do something? Did he say something to hurt you?" The protective mother in me prepared to give Manuel the tongue-lashing of his life for hurting her. Was there another woman, perhaps? I couldn't imagine him cheating after seeing them together and hearing her talk about him, but anything was possible.

"No. Yes. I don't know." Her voice broke. "It's complicated."

Her vague answer didn't tell me much. I didn't know if I should be angry at Manuel or not.

"Help me understand. Let me help you."

"You can't help." The words came out in a defeated voice. "No one can help. We were stupid to think we could make this work." She sniffled, rubbing a rough hand across her eyes.

"The two of you seemed perfect for each other."

She rolled over to face me, the devastation in her eyes making my breath catch. "*Seemed.* You and Mr. Harris might have been right. Manuel and I were rushing and don't know each other as well as we thought we did."

"But what happened?" I asked again.

Fresh tears spilled from the corners of her eyes. "I can't marry him. I just can't."

The finality in her voice worried me. It seemed there was no coming back from this.

"All right," I said, because what else could I say? I didn't want to keep pushing. "We don't have to talk about what happened right now."

I kicked off my shoes and lay down, wrapping my arms around her. She squeezed me tight, burying her face against my shoulder and sobbing like her heart was breaking. Which clearly it was.

I smoothed my hand over her short curls and murmured words of comfort.

"It's going to be okay," I whispered, though I had no idea if that was true. "We'll get through this."

Blossom continued crying, and I wished I could take away the pain like I used to when she was little and had a scraped knee or had bumped her elbow. No band-aid or kiss could chase away this pain.

All I could do was hold her and let her know she wasn't alone. So that's what I did until her tears stopped, her sobbing quieted, and she finally fell asleep. My poor baby.

I kissed her forehead and then carefully extracted myself from her arms. I placed a blanket over her and stood there for a moment, looking at her tear-streaked face.

Tears blurred my eyes. My baby was hurting, and I didn't know how to take away the pain.

I left her bedroom and closed the door softly behind me. In my own room, I checked my phone and saw multiple missed calls from Jamison. He had also sent three texts.

Jamison: Is she okay?

Jamison: Please call when you can.

Jamison: I'm worried.

I sank onto the side of the bed and called him, and he answered on the first ring.

"What happened?" he asked without greeting, his voice tight with concern.

"The wedding's off," I said, my voice breaking on the words. "She won't tell me why, but she's devastated, Jamison. I've never seen my daughter like this."

He didn't respond right away. Then he sighed. "Manuel isn't answering my calls."

Suddenly exhausted, I lay back on the bed and stared up at the ceiling fan. "She said she can't marry him and that you and I were right about them rushing. I have no idea what could possibly have happened to make her change her mind and suddenly listen to us. What if the problem—whatever it is—can't be fixed? Surely it can be fixed—right?"

"I wish I knew." He sounded as tired as I was. "We need to figure out what happened before we can help them. If Manuel screwed up..." He trailed off, muttering a curse under his breath.

"Look, it's late. We can touch base tomorrow. I want to spend as much time as possible with Blossom and find out what happened, so I probably won't see you tomorrow." Jamison and I usually saw each other on the weekend, but I couldn't leave Blossom alone in her state. "I'll call you when I can. Hopefully, you'll have a chance to talk to Manuel, and we can put our heads together about how to proceed."

"I'm going by his apartment tomorrow morning," Jamison said in a determined voice. "To make him tell me what happened. Call if you need me. Anytime."

"I will. I promise. We'll figure this out."

We hung up, and I remained on my back, staring up at the ceiling, my mind spinning with worry and questions.

The wedding was off, and I was devastated. I had gone through a complete mental shift since the night Blossom told me she was engaged. Manuel made my daughter happy, and because of my own deep feelings for Jamison, I understood how the two of them could have fallen in love and wanted to make a life together.

But there were no rules with love, and sometimes it wasn't destroyed by betrayal or outside forces. Sometimes it simply buckled under the weight of fear and doubt.

Chapter 29

Jamison

When Tallulah knocked on the door, I wasn't in the best mood. I had spoken to my son this morning and was even more distraught about the situation with him and Blossom now that I had more information.

When I opened the door, the raw energy I usually saw from Tallulah had dimmed. She wore jeans and a beautiful long-sleeved blouse, with her hair wrapped up in a colorful scarf. But she didn't look like herself. She appeared drawn and dispirited.

I pulled her into my arms, and she melted against me, her hands fisting the back of my shirt. We held onto each other for a while until I finally stepped back.

"How is Blossom?"

"Broken and upset, but I know the details now. She and I spoke this morning. Did you go to Manuel's apartment as planned?"

"Actually, he came here."

I took her hand and led her into the living room. We sat on my charcoal sofa, our legs touching, holding hands.

"What did he say?" she asked.

"He told me they went over budget on the wedding by a lot. Apparently, several thousand dollars, and he was stressed about dipping into his savings more than he had planned. Instead of coming to me or his mother, he decided to cover the expense himself."

"Because he wanted to prove he could handle the situation," Tallulah said quietly. "I can only imagine what he was thinking. He wanted to be responsible and to show that marrying Blossom wasn't a mistake."

Her words hit me in the chest.

"At least, that's what Blossom understood from their conversation," she continued. "She felt the same way and didn't want to ask me or her father for more money, but hated that they were over budget and she couldn't contribute to offset the overage. During her conversation with Manuel, he said he wished they had more of a cushion, which hurt her because she couldn't contribute without a job. The funny thing is, this past Sunday she told me there was an issue with the budget, but she downplayed the problem. Then the situation got worse."

"Worse how?" I asked.

Tallulah took a deep breath and slowly released it. "They went to the bank to set up a joint account, and the banker asked about their incomes."

I already knew where the conversation was going, and my stomach sank. "Manuel told me a little about the meeting. Let me guess, Blossom had to explain that she's currently unemployed."

Tallulah nodded. "The banker asked if she was actively interviewing. Manuel explained about her degree and how close she had come with a couple of positions, and then the banker made an offhand remark about how good it was that Blossom had Manuel's income to 'rely on.'"

I muttered a curse under my breath.

"She became upset. According to her, they argued in the car, and Manuel told her she was being dramatic and over-sensitive."

I winced. Those words sounded awfully close to something I would have said to his mother during one of our arguments. "So they fought about money, which we had argued about at Knife & Fork."

"Unfortunately, yes. Everything came to a head last night. Blossom told Manuel she didn't want to be a financial burden and wanted to contribute equally to the household. Instead of reassuring her, he became defensive—her words. He suggested that maybe you and I were right about them rushing, and perhaps they should have waited until they were more established."

"Manuel told me he panicked," I said quietly. "According to him, Blossom put words in his mouth and twisted everything he said, and he ended up saying things he didn't mean. One of which was that maybe they needed to take a long hard look at what they were doing."

"As far as my daughter was concerned, he basically told her that he was having second thoughts about her and the marriage."

"Manuel heard her accusations as her having second thoughts about *him*." Resting my elbows on my knees, I stared at the floor. "They're both protecting themselves and are too proud to back down."

"Sounds familiar," Tallulah said in a gentle but pointed voice.

I couldn't argue. Blossom and Manuel's fight sounded very similar to the ones my ex-wife and I used to have before our marriage completely fell apart. One of us defensive, both assuming the worst, and the walls going up instead of coming down.

"I know Manuel loves your daughter," I said, straightening. "When I saw him this morning, he obviously had been crying at some point." His appearance had shocked and wounded me. I wanted to take away his pain and fix his relationship. I had seen him cry as a child, but as a man, it was gut-wrenching in a different way.

As I listened to him recount what happened between him and Blossom, dread turned to guilt. Had I somehow caused the rift in their relationship? Had the comments I made because of my complicated history come back to haunt the kids?

"I'm sure Blossom loves him, but she seems certain they can't get past this."

We sat in silence for a while, both of us wrestling with the weight of what our children were going through.

"This is my fault," I said.

"No, it's not."

"It is. The first dinner we had together, I made comments about marriage being fifty-fifty and financial contributions, suggesting that they were rushing. I've always made comments to my son about having a partner who can contribute to the household." Guilt sat like acid in my gut. "My words planted doubts, and with the first sign of a problem, he resorted back to the things I said. I love Blossom, and I think she's a wonderful young woman. She's good for my son, and I'm sure I also made her doubt herself because I made her believe her only worth was contributing financially."

Tallulah took my hand. "You don't carry that burden alone. I certainly didn't help. I was so worried about them rushing because of my own failed marriage that I couldn't see they weren't making the same mistakes. I've made comments to Blossom over the past few months—about Manuel, whom I adore now because I see how good he is for her. They believed they were making the right decision until we made them doubt it."

"Until we made them doubt it," I agreed. "Now they believe one fight makes them fundamentally incompatible."

"We projected our pain and insecurities onto them."

Too agitated to sit any longer, I stood and paced to the window. I saw the parking lot, the landscaped grounds, and the normal Saturday afternoon activity of people going about their lives.

"For the record, Blossom is nothing like my ex-wife." I turned away from the view. "She's responsible and thoughtful and realistic and grounded. Anyone who hires her is going to be lucky."

Tallulah crossed one leg over the other. "Manuel is nothing like Karl. He's not dismissive or obsessed with structure."

"Our kids got the best of us, don't you think?"

"They did, and I believe they'll last. I had my doubts at first, but these two young people belong together. They're not too young, they didn't move too fast, and getting married is not too risky."

"We have to fix this," I said.

Tallulah stood and came toward me. She rested her hands on her hips. "I agree."

"Any ideas?"

She appeared thoughtful for a moment. "I have one."

Chapter 30

Tallulah

"Your mother is a hero," Mrs. Chen said to Blossom.

My daughter and I were at the counter of Far East Market. Chips for Blossom and drinks for both of us were on the counter.

"Stop," I said, slightly embarrassed.

"Do not be modest," my friend said, ringing up the purchases. "You saved all of our businesses. You should be proud. Have you already signed your new lease?"

"I did. How about you?"

"We did, and my husband is working on a frequent customer card for the partnership program. He is taking it very seriously."

"As he should. If planned right, it'll mean more business for the store. I'm working on my ideas. Julie wants to be included, and so does LaVon," I said, referring to the man who did reiki and reflexology in my center.

After chatting a bit more, we left. Mrs. Chen knew Manuel and Blossom had broken up, so she didn't mention the wedding, as she normally would have.

I unlocked the door to my store. "I really appreciate you helping me with this," I said. I let my daughter go ahead of me and closed the door without locking it again.

"It's fine, Mom. Not like I have anything else to do."

I placed the snacks on the counter, my heart hurting at her despondent tone.

She had been like this for the past four days, ever since she and Manuel called off the wedding. Hollow and simply going through the motions, her normally vibrant light had dimmed. Each time I looked at her, my heart broke a little bit more.

Which was exactly why Jamison and I had planned an intervention.

"The items are back here," I said.

I had told Blossom I needed her help with inventory that had been placed in the yoga room. I said I needed to go through everything so Julie could have the space.

When we walked in, Blossom looked around at the empty room with its polished bamboo floors. She frowned in confusion. "Where's the inventory? There's nothing here but mats."

"How odd. I should—"

"Hello?" a male voice called from the front.

Blossom's frown deepened.

"Sounds like Jamison," I said, pretending to be surprised. "Wait here. I'll be right back."

I escaped before she could respond, my heart hammering as I rushed to the front of the wellness center. Manuel and his father waited by the register.

"Hi Jamison, Manuel," I said.

"Hi, Ms. Washington."

"Are you doing okay?" I asked.

"Yeah." He gave a tight and brief fake smile.

"You said you needed help moving some boxes?" Jamison asked.

"I do, and I appreciate the two of you coming by to help. They're in the back."

They followed me, and as we approached the yoga room, I hung back and allowed Manuel to go ahead.

"In there," I said.

He stepped forward, and at the same time, Blossom looked up from her phone. Her entire body went rigid.

"Blossom."

Manuel's voice cracked on her name, and the longing in both of their faces was so obvious that I was confident Jamison and I had made the right decision. They loved each other. No doubt they loved each other.

"Mom, what's going on?"

Though she asked me the question, Blossom never took her eyes off Manuel. He hadn't taken his eyes off her, either.

"We brought you here to talk to each other," Jamison said. He moved to stand beside me, a couple of inches inside the room.

Blossom finally dragged her eyes from the man she loved. "We already said everything we needed to say days ago."

"Breaking up is not what you want," I said.

"You don't know what we want," Blossom said, but her voice wobbled.

"From where I'm standing, I see two people who are miserable without each other and are too afraid to admit they made a mistake."

The room fell silent. Blossom and Manuel made a point of not looking at one another.

I took a breath. "Jamison and I need a few minutes of your time, and we need you to listen to what we have to say."

Blossom folded her arms protectively across her torso, and Manuel shoved his hands into his pockets, his jaw tight, eyes trained on the floor.

I exchanged a glance with Jamison. This was it. We had to bring our A-game.

"The two of you are making a mistake by splitting up. You believe you're going to fail because of comments we made, but you're not."

"How can you be so sure?" Blossom asked.

"Because you love each other, and the fight you had is not really about money. The fight you had is about fear. Fear of pain. Fear of failure."

Jamison cleared his throat. "Love is terrifying, and it's risky, and there's no guarantee that things will work out. But I one hundred percent believe it's worth the risk and worth taking the leap because the alternative is moving through life and never finding out how much joy you can experience." When he finished talking, he looked at me. Those words were meant for me. "You can't plan love. It just happens on its own, whether or not you're ready. But that doesn't mean it's easy. When you love someone, you don't give up when the going gets tough. You work through your issues."

"Our marriages failed," I said, "but we both learned from our mistakes and realized we should've communicated instead of shutting down and avoiding the uncomfortable conversations. Instead of arguing, we should have listened. You have to talk to each other. You have to be honest with each other. You have to *listen* to each other. And for goodness' sake, don't throw away something real because you're afraid of what *might* happen. Fear should not dictate your choices."

"Here's the plan," Jamison began. "Tallulah and I are going to leave, and you're going to stay here and talk."

"What?" Blossom sounded panicked.

"We're not forcing you to do this," I said. "We're simply asking you to give yourselves a shot without distractions and emotions clouding the conversation. Decide together if you really want to end your relationship or if you want to work for your happiness. Jamison and I intervened and halted the cancellations. If you still want to call off the wedding after tonight, we'll give everyone a call in the morning and make the cancellations permanent."

Manuel turned to Blossom. "I'd like to stay and talk. How about you?"

She shrugged. "If you want to, I will."

I breathed easier. Progress.

"Sounds like we have a plan," Jamison said. He stepped through the open door, and I followed.

Before closing it, I looked at Manuel and Blossom. "We love you both, and whatever you decide, we'll support you. But we couldn't let you give up so easily."

"Thanks, Mom," Blossom said softly. A faint smile touched her lips. "For caring enough to poke your nose into my business."

"Yeah, thanks, Dad," Manuel added.

Jamison nodded. "Take all the time you need."

I closed the door, and Jamison and I walked to the front of the center in silence.

"What do you think?" I asked.

"I don't know." He rested against the counter and stuffed his hands into the pockets of his slacks. "We either nudged them in the right direction, or we made everything worse."

"Or we gave them permission to choose love instead of fear."

"Or that."

We stared at each other, hoping we had done right by our kids. All we could do was wait and trust we had truly seen love in their faces. Trust that the past few days of seeing them moping and despondent meant they needed each other.

"I appreciate you going along with my shenanigans," I said, stepping closer.

Jamison opened his arms, and I melted into him, wrapping my arms around his waist.

"You had a good idea. They needed to talk to each other before they threw away their future happiness."

"So what now?" I tilted my head back to look up at him.

"We wait." He paused, his gray eyes connecting with my brown ones in a speculative way. "And maybe we take our own advice."

"Isn't that what we've been doing?" I asked tentatively.

"Yes and no. What have you told Blossom about us?"

"She knows we care about each other."

"That's what you told her?"

"Yes. Because we do, right?"

"We do," he said in a careful voice, "but my feelings are deeper than simply caring for you. I've fallen in love with you, Tallulah, and if you haven't fallen in love with me yet, I plan to do everything I can to make sure you do."

My heart warmed at his words. "I have news for you. You don't have to do anything more. I'm already madly in love with you, for some odd reason."

He chuckled softly and kissed my forehead.

I closed my eyes and then placed my cheek against his chest. Being so close to him, being held in his embrace, was the highlight of my day. Unexpectedly, I had fallen for the kind of man I was certain I should avoid.

But love had a funny way of steamrolling over caution and proving fear was never wisdom to begin with.

Chapter 31

Tallulah

Blossom and Manuel's wedding couldn't have taken place on a better day. The September afternoon was warm enough that jackets hung forgotten on chair backs, but cool enough that the breeze carrying the scent of autumn did so without causing guests to shiver.

The venue, an old converted barn with exposed beams soaring overhead, glowed with vintage black lamps mounted on the walls. The wedding colors—burgundy, terracotta, and olive—transformed the space, adding warmth and rustic beauty to our surroundings.

After sitting for what seemed like an eternity, I stood near the edge of the space, watching my daughter dance salsa with one of Manuel's uncles—a man in his sixties who moved with amazing agility. Somehow, my daughter matched him step for step, her hips moving, her face radiant with joy.

Was this real life? My baby was married.

Hours after the ceremony, the reality of the day made me emotional. The same little girl who had trembled in my arms because she was terrified of thunder no longer needed me. She had a partner now who would be right by her side, and they would weather the storms of life together.

"Look at our little girl."

I had been so enthralled by my daughter and her dance partner that I hadn't noticed Karl coming to stand beside me. He held the remains of a taco from the food truck parked outside. He had shaved his beard, but his tawny skin bore the shadowy remnants of the facial hair he had worn for years, as if his skin were dyed with ink. His expression appeared softer than I'd seen in a long time.

"She's beautiful, isn't she?" I said.

"She sure is." He took the final bite of his taco and chewed thoughtfully. "Where did she learn to dance like that?"

"She and Manuel took salsa lessons."

"Huh." We watched Blossom spin under her partner's arm. "Her sense of adventure comes from you. Always willing to try new activities and jump into the unknown."

Surprised, I swung my head in his direction. I couldn't remember the last time he had paid me a compliment, particularly this kind. For most of our marriage, my willingness to try new things had been framed as impulsive, demonstrating a lack of planning.

Manuel made his way to the floor and cut in to claim his bride. Blossom melted into his arms as if they had been made to hold her.

"Manuel seems like a good kid," Karl commented.

"He is. I've gotten to know him well. He's responsible and quite wonderful, actually."

"And his father?" Karl's tone became extra neutral, but I caught the curiosity underneath. "You two seem... close."

Heat crept up my neck. I had barely spoken to Jamison all day, yet somehow Karl had picked up on our connection. Was it obvious to everyone that we were involved?

"We are close," I admitted.

"I figured." His gaze slid to me. "I hope he gets you. You deserve that. I never did understand your ways and kept trying to turn you into someone you weren't. I shouldn't have done that."

The admission hung between us. His honesty was overdue and strangely freeing.

"I appreciate you saying that. We both made mistakes, but we did a pretty good job with Blossom."

"I agree with you there." His smile was genuine, reminding me of the early days of our marriage, before our incompatibility became too big to ignore and crushed the lightness between us. "I should get back to my table. Laverne's probably wondering where I wandered off to."

"Tell her I said hi."

"I will." He disappeared across the room.

After a moment, I had the distinct impression I was being watched and noticed Jamison standing near the bar, talking to his older sister. They had the same gray eyes and dark hair. Though in conversation with his sibling, his attention remained locked on me.

He excused himself and crossed the space between us with his confident stride, hands casually tucked into the pockets of his pants. At some point, he had removed his jacket, and his shirt sleeves were rolled up to his forearms. My favorite look on him.

Damn, what a sexy man.

"Care to dance?" he asked when he reached me.

Salsa music pulsed through the barn, fast and rhythmic and well beyond my skill level. My eyes drifted to where Blossom and Manuel were moving together, surrounded by a crowd of family and friends who all seemed to know exactly which steps to take.

"Um, we didn't take salsa lessons, and I don't want to embarrass either of us," I told him.

My family called me Rhythmless Nation behind my back. No way was I getting on the dance floor.

"Are you scared?" Jamison taunted, amusement dancing in his eyes.

"I'm not *scared...*"

He arched an eyebrow. "Then dance like no one's watching."

"Salsa, though?" I eyed the dance floor with trepidation.

My mind spun with all the reasons I should decline. I could trip over my own feet. I might step on his toes. I would look ridiculous. People would notice. People would laugh.

Then I realized what I was doing.

I had fallen into an old trap, where I cared too much about other people's opinions. Where I chose safety over joy. Our kids had almost made the same mistake. I knew better. Even Jamison, a man who lived his life with rigid structure, who arrived everywhere early and planned his day down to the minute, knew better.

He held out his hand and rocked his hips from side to side in an exaggerated, epically unserious movement that made me burst out laughing.

God, I loved this man.

I placed my hand in his. "Let's do this."

He led me onto the dance floor, weaving a path through the friends and family twisting and turning more elegantly than I ever could. The music thrummed through the floorboards, up through my feet, encouraging me to let loose.

Jamison and I stepped into position and moved at the same time, bumping into each other.

I laughed, mortified. "Sorry. I—"

"One, two, three," he muttered under his breath.

We both moved at the same time again and nearly collided again. I laughed harder, the sound bubbling out of me in a helplessly unguarded way.

Shaking his head, Jamison's eyes crinkled at the corners with amusement.

"This is going well," I said.

He leaned forward, bringing his lips to my ear. "Let me lead."

And so I did. I relaxed, following instead of trying to steer. Our feet found the rhythm. Not perfectly. Not gracefully. But enough.

The music wrapped around us, the press of other bodies on the dance floor fading into obscurity. It was just me and Jamison, dancing to the sexy beat, his hand resting on my back in a reassuring way, melting my embarrassment into oblivion.

We weren't dancing salsa. We were just dancing. To our own beat. Our own rhythm. The one we had been working on for months—through cake tastings, yoga, dance lessons, late-night conversations, and an intervention to help our children trust themselves and their love.

"You're doing great," Jamison said, guiding me into a spin.

The song shifted into something slower, and the energy of the guests adjusted to fit the new tune. Couples edged closer as the frantic salsa rhythm gave way to a gentler sound. Jamison drew me in, and I willingly wrapped my arms around him and rested my head against his chest. I didn't care who knew we were together. This was my man, and I was publicly claiming him.

We danced until my feet—in heels I rarely wore—hurt. Then Blossom and Manuel cut the cake—a beautiful three-tier almond cake with Biscoff buttercream frosting—and zero cannabis.

Much later, after we had sent the couple off on their life

together, the food trucks were gone, the DJ had packed up, and only a handful of guests remained, Jamison and I sat at a table. My head rested on his shoulder as I watched a couple wrapped in each other's arms dance to their own private tune.

"Are you ready to go?" Jamison kissed the top of my head.

"Your place or mine?" I asked, stifling a yawn with my hand. I didn't want to leave, but my body was sending a message that it was time to go.

"Mine. I have real coffee. Not that mushroom coffee crap you had me drinking the other day."

I lifted my head from his shoulder. "It's good for you. It supports gut health and boosts your immune system, and the taste is similar to coffee."

"I don't drink coffee for the health benefits, and as a coffee aficionado, even in a blindfold test I'd know from the smell alone—before I took a sip—that slop isn't coffee. On this, you can't convert me."

I sighed. At least I had convinced him to drink tea on occasion after finally putting together a blend he liked.

Jamison stood and took my hand. "Come on."

He pulled me from the chair, and we walked hand in hand toward the door. His ex-wife and her husband were walking in the same direction.

"Good night," Maria said, shooting a knowing look at Jamison. She wore a colorful dress that cinched at the waist, her curly hair resting on her shoulders.

She and I had spoken earlier, and I liked her. Since she and Jamison had a good relationship, I wouldn't be surprised if she questioned him about me.

"Good night. Nice to meet you both," I said to her and her husband.

He was much less colorful than his wife and an accountant, if I remembered correctly. The Mexican version of Jamison.

Funny how we seemed to have a type, attracted to the same people despite our pasts.

"I'm probably going to fall asleep in the car," I warned as we strolled through the parking lot.

"I'll wake you when we get to my place."

The stars were out, bright and sparkling against the dark sky. We walked slowly, not in any hurry.

"Oh, Blossom received a job offer yesterday, which she accepted. For the position that made her late to the cake tasting."

"That's great!"

"I know. She's so happy, and I'm relieved she can relax and will be working in the field she has a degree in."

We stopped beside Jamison's car, and I squeezed his hand, my heart filled to overflowing. Our lives had taken an unexpected turn, one neither of us had planned. Our children had stepped into a future together, and now, without ceremony, we were stepping into ours.

Jamison kissed me—slow, deep, and full of promise. Then we climbed into the car and drove off into our future together.

Also by Delaney Diamond

More stories with mature couples!

Passion Rekindled (Brooks Family #2). Oscar Brooks has always assumed that his ex-wife hates him, but after an unplanned kiss, he's not so sure. Why does Sylvie Johnson always have such a hostile response to his presence? Is it love, or is it hate? He's determined to find out.

Seasoned. Three women. One summer. After three failed marriages, Renee Joseph is through with men, then things heat up with her neighbor. Right when Adelaide Flores is getting used to life without her ex-husband, they're thrown a curve ball that forces them together and reminds her of how much she still misses him. All her adult life, Jackie Bryant's happiness will depend on the tough decision she must make when her old lover, Tyson, comes back into her life.

Still in Love. Three years ago, Nadine Alesini divorced her husband and left Buenos Aires with her daughter in tow. Now she's back and forced to spend time with the man she left behind.

* * *

Audiobook samples and free short stories available at www.delaneydiamond.com.

About the Author

Delaney Diamond is the USA Today Bestselling Author of sensual, passionate romance novels. Originally from the U.S. Virgin Islands, she now lives in Atlanta, Georgia. She reads romance novels, mysteries, thrillers, and a fair amount of nonfiction. When she's not busy reading or writing, she's in the kitchen trying out new recipes, dining at one of her favorite restaurants, or traveling to an interesting locale.

Enjoy free reads on her website. Join her mailing list to get sneak peeks, notices of sale prices, and find out about new releases.

Join her mailing list
www.delaneydiamond.com

instagram.com/delaneydiamondbooks
x.com/DelaneyDiamond
pinterest.com/delaneydiamond

www.ingramcontent.com/pod-product-compliance
Lightning Source LLC
LaVergne TN
LVHW010057110826
845155LV00028B/378

* 9 7 8 1 9 4 6 3 0 2 3 3 5 *